WOODCUTTERS

Other Phoenix Fiction titles from Chicago

The Great Fire of London by Peter Ackroyd
The Bridge on the Drina by Ivo Andrić
Concrete by Thomas Bernhard
Gargoyles by Thomas Bernhard
The Lime Works by Thomas Bernhard
The Department by Gerald Warner Brace
Lord Dismiss Us by Michael Campbell
The Last, Long Journey by Roger Cleeve
Acts of Theft by Arthur A. Cohen
A Hero in His Time by Arthur A. Cohen
In the Days of Simon Stern by Arthur A. Cohen
Solomon's Folly by Leslie Croxford
The Old Man and the Bureaucrats by Mircea Eliade
Fish by Monroe Engel
In the Time of Greenbloom by Gabriel Fielding
The Birthday King by Gabriel Fielding
Through Streets Broad and Narrow by Gabriel Fielding
Concluding by Henry Green
Pictures from an Institution by Randall Jarrell
The Survival of the Fittest by Pamela Hansford Johnson
The Bachelor of Arts by R. K. Narayan
The English Teacher by R. K. Narayan
Swami and Friends by R. K. Narayan
Bright Day by J. B. Priestley
Angel Pavement by J. B. Priestley
The Good Companions by J. B. Priestley
Golk by Richard Stern
A Use of Riches by J. I. M. Stewart
The Painted Canoe by Anthony Winkler

WOODCUTTERS

THOMAS BERNHARD

Translated from the German by
David McLintock

THE UNIVERSITY OF CHICAGO PRESS

Published by arrangement with Alfred A. Knopf, Inc.

The University of Chicago Press, Chicago 60637

© 1987 by Alfred A. Knopf, Inc.
All rights reserved. Originally published 1987
University of Chicago Press edition 1989
Printed in the United States of America
98 97 96 95 94 93 92 91 90 89   5 4 3 2 1

Originally published in German as *Holzfällen* by Suhrkamp Verlag,
Frankfurt am Main. © 1984 by Suhrkamp Verlag.

Library of Congress Cataloging in Publication Data

Bernhard, Thomas.
  Woodcutters.

  (Phoenix fiction)
  Translation of: Holzfällen.
  Originally published: New York : Knopf, 1987.
  I. Title. II. Series.
PT2662.E7H6513 1989   833'.914   88-26076
ISBN 0-226-04396-7 (pbk.)

WOODCUTTERS

While everyone was waiting for the actor, who had promised to join the dinner party in the Gentzgasse after the premiere of *The Wild Duck*, I observed the Auersbergers carefully from the same wing chair I had sat in nearly every day during the fifties, reflecting that it had been a grave mistake to accept their invitation. I had not seen the couple for twenty years, and then, on the very day that our mutual friend *Joana* had died, I had met them by chance in the *Graben*, and without further ado I had accepted their invitation to this *artistic dinner*, as they described the supper they were giving. For twenty years I had not wanted to know anything about the Auersbergers; for twenty years I had not seen the Auersbergers, and in these twenty years the very mention of the name Auersberger had brought on third-degree nausea, I thought, sitting in the wing chair. And now this couple is bringing me face to face once more with the life we led in the fifties. For twenty years I've avoided the Auersbergers, for twenty years I haven't even met them, and then I have to run into them in the Graben, I thought.

It had been a piece of monumental folly not only to go to the Graben in the first place, but to walk up and down the Graben several times, as I was in the habit of doing, at least since returning to Vienna from London: it was a street where I might have known I would be *sure* to meet the Auersbergers one day, and not only the Auersbergers, but all the other people I had been avoiding for the last twenty or thirty years, people with whom I had had close ties in the fifties, what the Auersbergers used to call close *artistic ties*, ties which I had severed a quarter of a century ago, when I got away from the Auersbergers and went to London, *breaking*, as they say, with all my Viennese acquaintances of that period, not wanting to see them again or have anything more to do with them. Going for a walk in the Graben, I thought as I sat in the wing chair, means nothing more nor less than walking straight into the social hell of Vienna and meeting the very people I have no wish to meet, people whose sudden appearance brings on all kinds of physical and mental strains. Hence in recent years, whenever I came over from London to Vienna, I had chosen different routes for my walks, avoiding not only the Graben, but also the Kohlmarkt and, of course, the Kärntnerstrasse. I had avoided the Spiegelgasse, the Stallburggasse and the Dorotheergasse too, not to mention the dreaded Wollzeile and the Operngasse, where I have so often been trapped by the very people I most detest. But in recent weeks, I reflected as I sat in the wing chair, I had suddenly felt an urgent need to go to the Graben and the Kärntnerstrasse, because the air there was healthy, and because I suddenly found it pleasant to mingle with the morning crowds, both in the Graben *and* in the Kärntnerstrasse, and no doubt also because I wanted to escape from the months of solitude in my Währing apartment, to get away from the isolation that had begun to deaden my brain. In recent weeks I had always found it relaxing, both mentally and physically, to walk along the Kärntnerstrasse and the Graben, then back along the Graben and the Kärntnerstrasse. Walking back and forth like this was as beneficial to my mind as it was to my body, and in recent weeks I had walked up the Kärntnerstrasse and the Graben and back *every single day*, as though there were nothing I needed so much as just to walk up and down the Graben and the Kärntnerstrasse. It was in the Kärntnerstrasse and the Graben that I suddenly recovered my vitality and became myself again, after months of what I can only describe as mental and physical debility; walking along the Kärntnerstrasse and the Graben and back I felt refreshed. *All I need to do is to walk up and down like this,* I would think to myself, though that was not all I needed. Just to walk up and down, I kept on telling myself. And in fact it did enable me to start thinking again, even to philosophize, to take an interest once more in philosophy and literature, which had for so long been suppressed, even killed, within me. It was a mistake, as I now realize, to spend the winter in Vienna and not, like previous winters, in London, I thought, sitting in the wing chair. It was this long, sickening winter that killed off everything literary and philosophical there was inside me, and now I've made it all come back by walking up and down the Graben and the Kärntnerstrasse. And I actually attributed my Viennese mental condition, *my restored mental condition,* as I now felt able to call it, to the therapy I had first prescribed for myself in the middle of January, this Graben and Kärntnerstrasse therapy. This dreadful city of Vienna, I thought, having plunged me yet again into profound despair and utter hopelessness, has suddenly become the motor that enables my mind to function again as a living mind and my body as a living body; day by day I observed the progressive revival of mind and body, of everything inside me that had been dead during the whole of the winter; having blamed Vienna throughout the winter for my mental and physical atrophy, it was to Vienna that I now owed my restored vitality. I sat in the wing chair and silently paid tribute to the Kärntnerstrasse and the Graben, ascribing my mental and physical recovery solely to my Kärntnerstrasse and Graben therapy; and I told myself that I naturally had to pay a price for this therapy, and meeting the Auersbergers in the Graben, I thought, was the price of its success. It's a very high price, I thought, but it could have been much higher; after all I could have met much worse people in the Graben, for the Auersbergers aren't the worst people in the world, at least not the very worst. All the same it's bad enough to have met the Auersbergers in the Graben, I thought, sitting in the wing chair. A strong person, with strength of character to match, would have declined their invitation, I thought, but I'm not strong and I've no strength of character: on the contrary I'm the very weakest person, with the very weakest character, and that's what makes me more or less everyone's victim. And again I reflected that it had been a grave mistake to accept this couple's invitation: having resolved to have nothing more to do with them for the rest of my life, I cross the Graben, only to be accosted by them; they ask me whether I've heard about Joana's death, about her hanging herself, and then I go and accept their invitation. I momentarily gave way to the most shameful sentimentality, I thought, and the Auersbergers immediately took advantage of it; they took advantage of the suicide of our mutual friend Joana, I thought, to issue their invitation, which I at once accepted, though it would have been wiser to turn it down. But I didn't have the time, I thought, sitting in the wing chair: they *came up on me from behind* and told me what I already knew—that Joana had hanged herself at Kilb, at her parents' home—and then they invited me to dinner, to a *very artistic dinner*, they stressed—*all our friends from the old days*. They'd actually begun to walk on ahead of me when they issued their invitation, I thought, and they were already a few yards in front when I said *yes*, accepting their invitation and saying I'd come to their dinner party in this hideous apartment in the Gentzgasse. They were carrying a number of parcels, paper-wrapped parcels from various well-known shops in the center of the city, and they were wearing the same English overcoats they had worn thirty years before for shopping expeditions to the city center. Everything about them was what is called *shabby-genteel*. Actually *she did all the talking in the Graben: her husband, a composer in the Webern tradition* as he is described, didn't say a word to me, wishing to offend me by not speaking to me, I thought as I sat in the wing chair. They had said that they had no idea when Joana's funeral at Kilb would take place. I had been informed that day by a childhood friend of Joana's, just before I left home, that Joana had hanged herself. This friend, who runs a general store in Kilb, did not want to tell me over the telephone that Joana had *hanged* herself; she simply told me that she had *died*, but I told her outright that Joana had *not died*, but *killed herself*. She, as her friend, must know how she had done it, I said, but she simply would not tell me. Country people are more inhibited than townspeople about saying openly that *somebody has killed himself*, and they find it hardest of all to say how. I guessed at once that Joana had hanged herself; in fact I said to the woman from the general store, *Joana hanged herself, didn't she?* She was taken aback and simply said *Yes*. People like Joana hang themselves, I said. They don't throw themselves in the river or jump out of fourth-floor windows: they get a piece of rope, deftly tie a noose in it, attach it firmly to a beam, then let themselves drop into the noose. *Ballerinas and actresses hang themselves*, I told the woman from the general store. The fact that I had not heard from Joana for so long, I thought, sitting in the wing chair, had for some time struck me as suspicious, and I had often wondered lately whether Joana, a woman who had been deeply wounded, who had been cheated, deserted and scorned, might one day commit suicide. But in the Graben I had *pretended* to the Auersbergers that I knew nothing of Joana's suicide, feigning utter astonishment and shock, even though by eleven o'clock in the Graben I was no longer astonished or shocked by the tragedy, having heard about it at seven o'clock that morning; after walking up and down the Graben and the Kärntnerstrasse several times I found I was able to *endure* Joana's suicide, that I was able to bear it, in the bracing air of the Graben. Actually it would have been better had I not appeared utterly astonished by the Auersbergers' announcement of Joana's suicide; I should have told them that I had known about it for some time and that I even knew *how* she had killed herself. I ought to have told them the precise circumstances, I thought, and so deprived them of their triumph, which they were actually reveling in and savoring to the full, as I noted at the time while we were standing in front of Knizes'; for by pretending to know nothing whatever about Joana's death, by acting as though I had been stunned and shattered and dumb-founded by the terrible news, I had allowed the Auersbergers the thrill of being the sudden bearers of ill tidings, which naturally had not been my intention, though this was what I managed to achieve by my ineptitude, by claiming to know nothing whatever about Joana's suicide at the time of our meeting. All the time I was standing there with the Auersbergers I feigned ignorance, while knowing more or less everything about Joana's suicide. I did not know how they came to know that Joana had hanged herself, but the likelihood was that they too had been told by the woman from the general store. She would certainly have told them what she told me, I thought, though *not as much*; otherwise the Auersbergers would have told me more than they did about Joana's suicide. Of course they would be going to the funeral at Kilb, Auersberger's wife said, and she said it in a way which suggested that it would not be a matter of course for me to go to Joana's funeral; it was a kind of reproach, implying that I might possibly *not* go to Joana's funeral, that I might even find it convenient to avoid going to the funeral of our mutual friend, even though, like them, I had been on terms of the *most intimate friendship with her for so many years, indeed for decades.* The way she said it, I thought, was actually insulting, as was the fact that, after saying she would see me at Joana's funeral, she immediately went on to invite me to come to their so-called *artistic dinner* in the Gentzgasse the following Tuesday, that is, today, the day of Joana's funeral. It was in fact through Auersberger that I had first met Joana thirty years before, at a birthday party given for her husband in the Sebastiansplatz, in the Third District, a so-called *studio party* attended by nearly all the well-known artists of Vienna. Joana's husband was a so-called tapestry artist, a carpet weaver in other words, who had originally been a painter, and he had once won the first prize with one of his carpets at the Bienal in São Paulo in the mid-sixties. That Joana should commit suicide was the last thing they would have expected, the Auersbergers had said in the Graben, and before rushing off with all their parcels they told me that they had bought *everything by Ludwig Wittgenstein*, so that they could *immerse themselves in Wittgenstein during the coming weeks.* They've probably got Wittgenstein in the smallest parcel, I thought, the one dangling from her right arm. And again I reflected that it had been a grave error to accept the Auersbergers' invitation, considering how I detest all such invitations, and how for so many years I had avoided invitations to *artistic dinners* of this kind, having attended so many of them until I was well into my forties. I was thoroughly familiar with what they were like—and I know of scarcely anything more repugnant. Actually these Auersberger invitations haven't changed, I thought, sitting in the wing chair: they're just the same as they were in the fifties, when they not only bored me to death, but drove me half demented. For twenty years you've detested the Auersbergers, I told myself, sitting in the wing chair, and then you run into them in the Graben and accept their invitation, and you actually turn up in the Gentzgasse at the appointed time. What's more, you know all the others who've been invited to this dinner party, and still you turn up. And it struck me that I would have done better to spend this evening—or rather this whole night— reading Gogol or Dostoevski or Chekhov, rather than to come to this hateful dinner party in the Gentzgasse. The Auersbergers are the people who destroyed your existence, your very life, I told myself, sitting in the wing chair; they were the people who, in the early fifties, drove you into such an appalling mental and physical state, into what amounted to an existential crisis, into a state of such complete helplessness that you ended up in the Steinhof mental clinic, yet you still had to come here tonight. If you hadn't turned your back on them at the crucial moment you'd have been annihilated. First they'd have destroyed you, then they'd have annihilated you. If I'd stayed with them only a few days longer at Maria Zaal, I thought, sitting in the wing chair, it would have been certain death. They'd have squeezed you dry, I told myself as I sat in the wing chair, and then discarded you. You run into your ghastly destroyers and murderers in the Graben, and in a momentary access of sentimentality you let yourself be invited to the Gentzgasse—and you actually turn up, I said to myself as I sat in the wing chair. And again it struck me that I would have done better to read my Pascal or my Gogol or my Montaigne, or play some Satie or Schönberg on the piano, even though my old piano is so badly out of tune. You walk to the Graben, to get some fresh air and recoup your vitality, and run straight into the arms of your former destroyers and annihilators, and you even tell them how much you're looking forward to the evening, to their *artistic dinner*, which can't be anything but dreary, like all their dinner parties, like all the evenings you can recall spending with them. Only a half-wit devoid of all character could accept an invitation like that, I thought, sitting in the wing chair. It's now thirty years since they lured you into their trap and you let yourself be caught. It's thirty years since these people subjected you to daily indignities and you abjectly submitted to them, I thought as I sat in the wing chair—thirty years since you more or less *sold* yourself to them in the most despicable fashion, thirty years since you played the fool for them, I thought, sitting in the wing chair. And it's twenty-six years since you escaped from them—at the last possible moment. For twenty years you haven't set eyes on them, and then, all unsuspecting, you go for a walk in the Graben and fall right into their hands; you let yourself be invited to the Gentzgasse, and, what's more, you actually turn up, and you even tell them you're looking forward to their *artistic dinner*, I thought, sitting in the wing chair. Auersberger's wife was talking incessantly about the *superb actor* who had reached the peak of his career in the new production of *The Wild Duck*. Meanwhile the guests, having arrived two hours before midnight, consoled themselves with one bottle of champagne after another; every fifteen minutes the hostess circulated among them to replenish the glasses which all these more or less distasteful people held out to her. She was wearing the yellow dress I knew so well. Possibly she's put it on *specially for me*, I thought, because thirty years ago I used to compliment her on this dress, which at the time I thought looked extremely good on her, though now I did not find it at all becoming—on the contrary I actually found it taste-less—and which now had a black velvet collar instead of the red one it had had thirty years ago. She kept repeating the words *a superb actor* and *a fascinating production of The Wild Duck* in that voice of hers which even thirty years ago used to grate on me, though thirty years ago I had thought it an interesting voice, even if it did grate, whereas now I found it simply vulgar and repellent. The way she said *altogether the most important actor* and *the greatest living actor* I found quite unendurable. I never could stand her voice, but now that it was old and cracked and carried a permanent undertone of hysteria—now that it was strained and worn out, as they say of singers—I found it quite insupportable. This was the voice, I reflected, that used to sing Purcell and the *Songbook of Anna Magdalena*

Bach, and when her husband, who was my friend (and whom the experts always called a composer in the Webern tradition), accompanied her at the Steinway it used to bring tears to my eyes. I was twenty-two at the time and in love with everything that Maria Zaal and the Gentzgasse stood for; I even used to write poems. But now I was sickened at the thought of the loathsome scenes I had been quite happy to take part in thirty years earlier. I would accompany the Auersbergers as they moved back and forth between Maria Zaal and the Gentzgasse every two weeks, continually switching between their two residences, I thought as I sat in the wing chair, having drunk several glasses of champagne in a very short time. Observing the Auersbergers from my wing chair, I recalled that it was she who had spoken to me in the Graben, not her husband. And you immediately accepted her invitation! *They came up from behind and spoke to you,* I told myself; they'd probably been *observing you from behind* for some time, *following you and observing you,* and then *suddenly, when the time was ripe,* they addressed you. Sitting in the wing chair, I recalled that thirty years earlier I had once seen Auersberger —who incidentally has been drunk for the last thirty years— walking along the Rotenturmstrasse with a woman I did not know, a woman of about forty who looked thoroughly dissipated and was obviously down at heel, with long hair and worn-out leather boots. I observed everything about him and his companion fairly thoroughly, wondering all the time whether I should speak to him or not, but in the end I did not speak to him. My instinct told me, You mustn't speak to him; if you do he'll make some offensive remark that will demoralize you for days. And so I refrained: I controlled myself and observed him all the way down to the Schwedenplatz, where he and the woman disappeared into an old house that was due for demolition. All the time I could not take my eyes off his revolting legs, clad in coarse-knit knee-length stockings, his oddly perverted rhythmical gait, and the bald patch at the back of his head. He seemed a good match for his seedy companion, who was doubtless an artiste of some kind, a worn-out singer or a low-class unemployed actress, I thought as I sat in the wing chair. Sitting in the wing chair, I recalled how I had turned around, quivering with revulsion, and set off toward the Stephansplatz after the pair had disappeared into that dilapidated building. I was so sickened by what I had just witnessed that I turned to throw up against the wall in front of the *Aida* coffeehouse; but then I looked into one of the mirrors of the coffeehouse and found myself staring at my own dissipated face and my own debauched body, and I felt more sickened by myself than I had been by Auersberger and his companion, so I turned around and walked as fast as I could in the direction of the Stephansplatz and the Graben and the Kohlmarkt. Finally, as I now recalled in the wing chair, I reached the café *Eiles*, where I fell upon a pile of newspapers in order to forget the sight of Auersberger and his companion and my encounter with myself. This trick of going to the café *Eiles* had always worked. I would go in, get myself a pile of newspapers, and recover my composure. Nor did it have to be the café *Eiles*: the *Museum* or the *Bräunerhof* also produced the desired effect. Just as some people run to the park or the woods in search of calm and distraction, I have always run to the coffeehouse. Thus it was as likely as not, I reflected in the wing chair, that before finally addressing me the Auersbergers had observed me for some time, just as closely as I had observed Auersber-

ger that day in the Rotenturmstrasse, and no doubt with
the same ruthlessness, the same monstrous inhumanity. We
learn a great deal, I reflected in the wing chair, if we observe people from behind when they are unaware of being
observed, observing them for as long we can, prolonging
our ruthless and monstrous observation for as long as possible without addressing them, keeping control of ourselves and refraining from speaking to them, then being
able simply to turn on our heel and walk away from them,
in the truest sense of the phrase—if we have the skill and
the cunning that I displayed that day at the bottom of the
Rotenturmstrasse, when I turned on my heel and walked
away. We should apply this observation procedure both to
people we love and to people we hate, I thought, sitting in
the wing chair and observing Auersberger's wife, who kept
glancing at the clock and trying to console her guests for
having to wait for supper so long, that is to say until the
actor made his entrance. I had once seen this actor at the
Burgtheater, many years before, in one of those emetic
English society farces the inanity of which is tolerable only
because it is English inanity and not the German or Austrian variety, and which have been put on at the Burgtheater
again and again with appalling regularity over the past
quarter of a century, because during this time the Burgtheater has made a specialty of English inanity and the
Viennese public has grown accustomed to it. I remembered
him as a so-called matinee idol, one of the theatrical dandies
who own villas in Grinzing or Hietzing and pander to the
sort of Austrian theatrical imbecility that has its home in
the Burgtheater, one of the mindless hams who, over the
last quarter of a century, have collaborated with all the
directors appointed to the *Burg*, as it is affectionately called,

to turn it into a thoroughly brainless institution dedicated to ranting and the murder of the classics. The Burgtheater has been artistically bankrupt for so long, I thought, sitting in the wing chair, that it is impossible to say precisely when it went into liquidation, and the actors who make their nightly appearances there are the bankrupts. Nevertheless, to invite one of these barnstormers to supper, to a so-called *artistic dinner*, I thought, sitting in the wing chair and observing the Auersbergers and their guests, is still regarded by people like the Auersbergers who own apartments in the Gentzgasse as something out of this world. It's a peculiarly Austrian perversion, I thought, sitting in the wing chair, and I realized just what a special occasion this must be for the Auersbergers, when supper was delayed for over an hour after it was due to be served, in other words until half past twelve, when the doorbell would finally ring and the actor would make his appearance at the Auersbergers' apartment in the Gentzgasse, signaling his entrance with the ostentatious clearing of the throat that Burgtheater actors affect. Secretly I have always detested actors, and those who perform at the Burgtheater have always earned my special detestation—except of course for the very greatest, like Wessely and Gold, for whom I have always had the profoundest affection—and the one whom the Auersbergers had invited to the Gentzgasse that evening was unquestionably one of the most objectionable specimens I have met. Born in the Tyrol and having, in the course of three decades, *acted his way into the hearts of the Viennese by his performances in Grillparzer* (as I once saw it expressed), he is for me the personification of the anti-artist, I thought, sitting in the wing chair; he's the archetypal mindless ham, who's always been popular at

the Burgtheater and in Austria generally, utterly devoid
of imagination and hence of wit, one of those unspeakable
emotionalists who tread the boards of the Burgtheater every
evening in droves, wringing their hands in their unnatural
provincial fashion, falling upon whatever work is being
performed, and clubbing it to death with the sheer brute
force of their histrionics. For decades, I thought as I sat
in the wing chair, these people have annihilated everything
with their mimic muscle-power. It's not only the gentle
Raimund and the sensitive Kleist who get beaten to a pulp
at the Burgtheater, which fancies it's taken a perpetual
lease on the theatrical art: even the great Shakespeare falls
victim to the butchers of the Burgtheater. But in this country, I thought, sitting in the wing chair, the Burgtheater
actor is regarded as a superior being, and to have so much
as a nodding acquaintance with an actor from the Burgtheater, to say nothing of having one to supper in one's
apartment, is regarded by the Austrians, and above all by
the Viennese, as an unparalleled honor. Yet to me, I thought
as I sat in the wing chair, this has always made the Austrians,
and above all the Viennese, appear ridiculous, whether
they lay claim to a slight personal acquaintance with an
actor from the Burgtheater or tell you that they have even
had one to supper. These actors are petit bourgeois nonentities who know nothing whatever about the art of the
theater and have long since turned the Burgtheater into a
hospice for their terminal dilettantism. It was not for nothing, I thought, that back in the fifties I chose this particular wing chair, which still stands in the same place, though
the Auersbergers have since had it re-covered. Sitting here,
I can see and hear everything—nothing escapes me. I was
wearing my so-called *funeral suit*, which I bought twenty-

three years ago in Graz, on my way to Trieste, and which
is now far too tight for me. I had worn it to Joana's funeral
at Kilb, which did not end until late. in the afternoon. As
I sat there I reflected that once more, contrary to my better
judgment, I was making myself cheap and contemptible,
having accepted the Auersbergers' supper invitation instead
of declining it. That day in the Graben I had momentarily
become soft and weak and so acted contrary to my nature,
and tonight I was standing not only my character, but
my whole nature, on its head. Only Joana's suicide could
have prompted such an irrational reaction. Had I not been
so devastated by her suicide, I would naturally have declined the invitation, I now thought, sitting in the wing
chair, when the Auersbergers issued it in that abrupt, direct
manner of theirs, employing their customary surprise tactics,
which I've always found so distasteful. Almost all the supper
guests were still in their funeral attire, I noted, sitting in the
wing chair; only one or two had changed for the party,
and so nearly everybody was dressed in black, looking just
as exhausted as I was from the strain of what we had been
through at Kilb, where it had actually rained heavily during
the ceremony. And naturally their sole topic of conversation, of which I caught only snatches, was Joana's funeral
and *the tragedy of her life*, which had been brought on by
her husband's walking out on her seventeen or eighteen
years earlier and going off to Mexico. One or two tapestries hung on the Auersbergers' walls—the work of this
self-same husband who, they all said, had Joana's suicide
on his conscience—and as they hung there, accusing their
creator, they darkened the scene, which was in any case
only dimly lit by a number of Empire-style lamps. The
tapestry artist had bolted to Mexico with, of all people, his
wife's best friend, as I heard people recall more than once

in the semidarkness of the Gentzgasse, leaving the *unhappy Joana* all alone. To Mexico of all places, and at the very moment when it was bound to be a *mortal blow* to her. Left alone at forty, in the studio in the Sebastiansplatz, with no financial support, with virtually nothing. More than once I heard somebody say that it was surprising Joana had not hanged herself in the studio in the Sebastiansplatz, rather than at her parents' home in Kilb—that she had chosen to do it in the country and not in the city. Several times I heard somebody remark that it was homesickness that had driven her to Kilb, away from Vienna, away from the *urban quagmire* to the *rural idyll*. I actually heard somebody use the phrases *urban quagmire* and *rural idyll*, not without a malignant undertone; I think it was Auersberger who kept on repeating them as I sat in the wing chair observing his wife, who was constantly bursting into hysterical laughter, trying to keep everybody's spirits up until the actor made his entrance. The apartment, on the third floor of the house, consists of seven or eight rooms filled with Josephine and Biedermeier furniture. It formerly belonged to Auersberger's parents-in-law. His wife's father, a rather feeble-minded physician from Graz, had his consulting room here in the Gentzgasse, though he never made a career as a doctor. Her mother, an unshapely, chubby-cheeked creature from the rural gentry of Styria, permanently lost her hair at the age of forty after being treated for influenza by her husband, and prematurely withdrew from society. She and her husband were able to live in the Gentzgasse thanks to her mother's fortune, which derived from the family estates in Styria and then devolved upon *her*. She provided for everything, since her husband earned nothing as a doctor. He was a socialite, what is known as a beau, who went to all the big Viennese balls during the carnival season and throughout his life was able to conceal his stupidity behind a pleasingly slim exterior. Throughout her life Auersberger's mother-in-law had a raw deal from her husband, but was content to accept her modest social station, not that of a member of the nobility, but one that was thoroughly petit bourgeois. Her son-in-law, as I suddenly recalled, sitting in the wing chair, made a point of hiding her wig from time to time—whenever the mood took him—both in the Gentzgasse and at Maria Zaal in Styria, so that the poor woman was unable to leave the house. It used to amuse him, after he had hidden her wig, to drive his mother-in-law up the wall, as they say. Even when he was going on forty he used to hide her wigs—by that time she had provided herself with several—which was a symptom of his sickness and infantility. I often witnessed this game of hide-and-seek at Maria Zaal and in the Gentzgasse, and I honestly have to say that I was amused by it and did not feel in the least ashamed of myself. His mother-in-law would be forced to stay at home because her son-in-law had hidden her wigs, and this was especially likely to happen on public holidays. In the end he would throw her wigs in her face. He needed his mother-in-law's humiliation, I reflected, sitting in the wing chair and observing him in the background of the music room, just as he needed the triumph that this diabolical behavior of his brought him. I was revolted to see Auersberger practicing a simple finger exercise on the piano, raising his pale face, which was already glassy and vacant as a result of the alcohol he had consumed, and sticking the tip of his tongue out of his tiny mouth, which by now had a bluish tinge. He's chosen Giovanni Gabrieli for this sick little scene, I thought. And I recalled that at the time when my friendship with the Auersbergers was at its most intense, I would often stand by the Steinway and sing Italian, German and English arias—grossly overrating my talent, as I now realize. I had completed my studies at the Mozarteum, the so-called academy of music and performing arts in Salzburg, though I never took advantage of my musical training; I had left the Mozarteum as a deep bass-baritone, with no prospect, and indeed no intention, of becoming a performing artist. But at Maria Zaal the afternoons were long, and in the Gentzgasse the afternoons and nights were equally long; and so virtually every day Auersberger would sit down at his grand piano, with me standing beside him, and in the course of several weeks, as I now recalled, sitting in the wing chair, we would work our way through the whole classical repertoire of arias and *Lieder*. Auersberger, whom I once called the *Novalis of sound*, had always been a first-class pianist, I thought, sitting in the wing chair, and even now, drunk though he is, he would need to sit at the Steinway for no more than two or three minutes to prove his artistry. But he's gone to seed, I thought, sitting in the wing chair; through years of alcoholic addiction he's allowed everything within him to degenerate, even his musical talent, which he once prized above all else. We may know for decades that someone close to us is a ridiculous person, but it's only after a lapse of decades that we suddenly *see* it, I thought, sitting in the wing chair, just as I'm suddenly seeing now, with absolute clarity, that Auersberger (the so-called successor of Webern) is a ridiculous person. And just as Auersberger, who's continually drunk, is ridiculous in his own way, and probably always has been, I thought, sitting in the wing chair, so too his wife is ridiculous and always has been. You used to be in love with these ridiculous people, I told myself as I sat in the wing chair, head over heels in love with these ridiculous, low, vicious people, who suddenly saw you again after twenty years, in the Graben of all places, and on the very day Joana killed herself. They came up and spoke to you and invited you to attend their *artistic dinner party with the famous Burgtheater actor* in the Gentzgasse. What ridiculous, vicious people they are! I thought, sitting in the wing chair. And suddenly it struck me what a low, ridiculous character I myself was, having accepted their invitation and nonchalantly taken my place in their wing chair as though nothing had happened—stretching out and crossing my legs and finishing off what must by now have been my third or fourth glass of champagne. And I told myself that I was actually far more base and vicious than the Auersbergers. They caught you out with their invitation, and you promptly accepted it, I told myself. Though they were all waiting for the actor, everybody was *obsessed* with Joana's suicide, and also with her funeral, which had taken place that afternoon and had clearly left its mark on them. As I sat in the wing chair, waiting like all the others until well after midnight for the actor to arrive, I could think of nothing but Joana's appalling funeral, of the events that had led up to it, of the reasons for the utter despair that had driven her to take her life. Sitting in the wing chair, I was left undisturbed, since it stood behind the door through which the guests entered the apartment, and in the semidarkness of the anteroom I was able to devote myself to the thoughts and fantasies that occupied my mind. When guests arrived they did not recognize me until after they had walked past me, and then only if they happened to turn around after entering the apartment, which very few of them did: most of them went straight through the anteroom to the music room, the door of which was always kept open. For as far back as I can remember, the door between the anteroom and the music room has never been closed; I can remember that even when the Auersbergers had nobody but me staying with them they never closed the door to the music room, because with the door open the room had excellent acoustics, something to which Auersberger, being a composer, naturally attached the greatest importance. From my vantage point in the wing chair I could see the people in the music room without their seeing me. They all walked straight from the entrance to the music room. This was how it had always been, and on this evening the guests seemed positively to race through the anteroom and into the music room, where Auersberger's wife was waiting to welcome them with arms outstretched, as though it was to *her* that condolences were due for Joana's death, as though *she* was now exploiting Joana's death for her own purposes. Since most of them had already seen one another that afternoon at Kilb, they contented themselves with a brief embrace, after which they each sat down with a glass of champagne in one of the chairs in the music room. While Auersberger's wife went on and on about the *great actor*, this *supremely great actor*, this *incomparable actor*, this *genius of an actor*, the guests could be heard almost continually uttering the name *Joana*. The name had always sounded good, but it was only her professional name. In reality she was plain *Elfriede Slukal* from Kilb, and it never did her any good to call herself Joana; she did so in the hope of making a career for herself in Vienna, but she never made a career. Having gone from Kilb to Vienna, without the slightest idea of what to do next, she had been advised by a former dancer and choreographer, who had once choreographed a ballet at the State Opera, to take the name *Joana*, which had an exotic ring to it—at any rate in Vienna. *Little Elfriede,* as her mother used to call her, at once acted upon this advice, hoping that as Joana she could make a career for herself that would have been impossible for someone called Elfriede, let alone Elfriede Slukal. But it was a grave miscalculation, I thought, sitting in the wing chair: there was obviously no career for Elfriede Slukal, even under the name Joana, but that evening in the Gentzgasse, all the guests at the *artistic dinner* uttered the name Joana as though some human miracle lay concealed behind it. To judge by what I heard from my wing chair, they all spoke of Joana's *death*, not of her *suicide*, and I did not once hear the word *hanged*. By now some sixteen or seventeen guests must have arrived for this *artistic dinner*, I thought, sitting in the wing chair. I knew most of them, and nodded to them without getting up. Five or six of them were strangers to me, and two of these appeared to be young writers. I have a gift for behaving in such a way that people leave me alone whenever I wish, and as I sat in the wing chair I showed myself to be a past master in the art of being left alone; people recognized me in the half-light of the anteroom and tried to strike up a conversation, but I at once deterred them simply by remaining seated and pretending not to understand what they said, and then, at precisely the right moment, looking down at the ground instead of into their faces. I behaved as though I were still completely taken up with Joana's suicide, sitting in the wing chair and affecting an absent-minded air whenever there was a risk that one of the guests might take it into his head to keep me company, which was something I was determined to prevent. I was willing to risk being thought unfriendly, even ill-mannered, if not downright offensive; it is quite contrary to my nature to behave badly in company, but I have to confess that on this occasion my behavior was impolite, dismissive and hostile.

Some of the guests had already heard about my notorious strangeness and oddity, what somebody once called my *dangerous eccentricity*; I had even been told that my years in London had produced in me a *quite disturbing madness*. People hated me and everything I wrote, and ganged up against me in the most vicious fashion whenever they saw me. But ever since my return from London I had been on my guard against them, against all the people I had known previously, but above all against these so-called *artistic figures from the fifties,* and especially those who had come to this *artistic dinner*. As soon as they entered the apartment they more or less fell into my trap, behaving as though they were unobserved, while in fact I was observing them intently from my wing chair. They walked over to Auersberger's wife, who was standing by the door of the music room, and let themselves be embraced. They were all without exception consummate performers who knew how to get the maximum mileage out of the *Joana Case*. The Auersbergers had always been, at least ostensibly, what are called *good hosts*; they were uniquely and uninhibitedly liberal in their mania for throwing parties and in their endless zeal for things artistic and cultural, and so they were forever hunting down celebrities. It has to be admitted that, dreadful and distasteful though they were, they had a fair measure of what is called *Austrian charm*. But the fact that I accepted their invitation wasn't due to their *Austrian charm*, I thought as I sat in the wing chair, but to the insolent way they issued it without warning that day in the Graben; and I watched Auersberger sitting at the Steinway, leaning forward because of his shortsightedness and leafing through some music, which I eventually recognized as the *Anton von Webern Album* I knew so well. He was sorting out the music for a short recital to be

given by his wife. Curiously enough, I've managed to keep
my sight up to now, I thought, sitting in the wing chair,
though I've reached an age when many people rapidly
become farsighted; a lot of people begin to lose their sight
in their mid-forties, suddenly finding that they have to
hold the newspaper a couple of feet away from them in
order to read it. I was still spared any such impairment
of vision; I could now see better than ever, I thought, more
sharply and ruthlessly than ever, with London eyes, it
would seem. The champagne the Auersbergers are serving
this evening isn't absolutely the best in the world, I thought,
sitting in the wing chair, but all the same it's one of the
three or four most expensive—no doubt what they deem
appropriate to mark the visit of an actor from the Burgtheater. Naturally I had sweated a good deal at Joana's
funeral, and, not wishing to change for this *artistic dinner*,
I had sprayed cologne on my clothes—rather too freely,
it now occurred to me. I have always found it unpardon-
able to turn up stinking of cologne, but this evening the
stench was not noticeable: to judge by the atmosphere in
the Auersbergers' apartment, they had all splashed too
much scent on their clothes. Every now and then I saw
the cook appear from the kitchen and stick her head around
the door of the music room to find out whether she could
start serving supper, but the actor had still not arrived.
Auersberger's wife was now sitting in one of those slender
Empire chairs whose backs consist simply of a lyre carved
out of walnut, doing her best to keep the guests happy.
Most of them were smoking and, like me, drinking champagne, while at the same time nibbling at the snacks that
the hostess had disposed all around the apartment in little
dishes made of fine Herend porcelain. There was one next

to me, but having always had an equal dislike for Herend porcelain and pre-dinner snacks, I did not eat any. I have never been partial to savory snacks, and certainly not to the Japanese variety that it has recently become fashionable to serve at all Viennese receptions. It really is an impertinence, I said to myself, to make us all wait for the actor, to demean all the guests, including myself, by turning us into a stage set for this man from the Burgtheater. At one point Auersberger remarked that he detested the theater. Whenever he had had more to drink than his wife permitted, he would suddenly reveal his innermost self, and on this occasion he suddenly started inveighing against the actor, who had not even arrived, calling the Burgtheater a *pigsty* (admittedly not without justification) and the actor himself a *megalomaniac cliché-monger*, but his wife immediately rebuked him, rolling her eyes and telling him to go back to the piano where he belonged and keep quiet. They haven't changed, I said to myself, sitting in the wing chair: she's anxious to preserve the harmony of her *artistic dinner*, and he's threatening to destroy it. They're both committed to the same ends, the same social ends, I thought, but late in the evening he puts on a show of wanting to escape, remembering what he owes himself, so to speak, as an artistic personality. Essentially they're both completely taken up with society, I thought, without which they couldn't exist—the higher reaches of society of course, because they've never been able to make it to the highest—while on the other hand they've never abandoned their artistic pretensions, their links with Webern, Berg, Schönberg and the rest, which they've always felt obliged to harp on at every opportunity in their craze for social recognition. Joana wasn't Auersberger's best friend, as people often said, but she certainly was the *one* artistic friend he had, I thought as I sat in the wing chair, and it was through him, as I have said, that I first met her at the studio in the Sebastiansplatz. Joana was a country girl who had been spoiled by her mother, the wife of a railroad worker in Kilb; her parents anticipated her every wish, and if possible fulfilled it. This was certainly *one* of the reasons for her suicide, it now struck me—this continual *pampering* which goes on in the families of small country tradesmen, especially in Lower Austria. What a beautiful village Kilb is! I thought. I've spent many afternoons and evenings there, and sometimes even stayed the night; the Slukals, Joana's parents, often could not put me up in their little one-story house, which, though damp, was always cozy, and so on those occasions I would stay at the local inn, which was called the *Iron Hand*. I would spend hours walking with Joana, discussing the art of dance and the so-called *movement studio* she ran in Vienna. From her very earliest childhood, when she was still at the elementary school in Kilb, Joana had wanted to become famous either as an actress or as a ballerina—she was never sure which. Finally she decided to call herself a *choreographer*, and arranged appearances for herself in a number of plays based on fairy tales, which were staged in various small Viennese theaters. She got extremely favorable press notices and finally succeeded in putting on a *deportment class* at the Burgtheater. It was utterly futile, of course, to imagine that she could teach deportment to the actors at the Burgtheater: they could no more be taught how to deport themselves than they could be taught how to speak. In the mid-fifties, however, through the good offices of a senior official in the Burgtheater management, she was engaged to coach the actors in the art of deportment. This was a failure because the actors showed absolutely no interest and because in the end she lost interest too. Yet for a whole year she got a decent fee for her efforts. Basically she could never make up her mind whether she wanted to be an actress or a ballerina; and so she had danced and acted throughout her childhood, and when she went to Vienna she actually studied drama at the Reinhardt Seminar, where she finally qualified, though no theater ever engaged her. At the height of her indecision, which she constantly referred to as her *artistic crisis*, she married the carpet designer, the *tapestry artist* as she used to call him, I recalled, sitting in the wing chair. For over ten years Joana and her tapestry artist lived in the Third District, in a patrician house in the Sebastiansplatz that had been built in 1880. Here they occupied a penthouse studio with a thousand square feet of floor space under three enormous glass domes. It was beneath these domes that he wove the tapestries that made him famous— and not just in Europe. Coming from an old Jewish family and having started out as a painter, he always averred that the art of weaving, in other words tapestry making, had been the *saving* of him. He ran into Joana at just the right moment, for it was her freshness and beauty that very soon turned the studio in the Sebastiansplatz into one of the artistic centers of Viennese society. He wove the tapestries and she sold them. It was Joana's charm that made the works of her tapestry artist famous, first in Vienna, then in Europe, and finally in America, I thought as I sat in the wing chair, and at once I recalled that it was at the height of his fame (which he undoubtedly owed to Joana!) that he bolted, as they say, with his wife's best friend and ended up in Mexico. They married in Mexico City, but he divorced his new wife only a year later to marry a Mexican (the daughter of a Mexican minister!), to whom he is still married. Joana really was an *unlucky creature*, from the day she was born until the day she died, I thought, sitting in the wing chair. And it was on the very day Joana killed herself that I went to the Graben and ran into the Auersbergers—I don't believe that was pure chance, I thought, sitting in the wing chair. For ten years I didn't bother about Joana, I thought; I completely lost sight of her for years and didn't hear anything more of her. And today at Kilb I learned that during the last few years of her life she had had what is called a *constant companion*, a second companion in other words; I saw this man for the first time at the *Iron Hand*, I thought, a Carinthian from the Gail Valley, who made a continual effort to speak standard German, though it came across as the most pathetic variety of standard German I've ever heard. This man had put on an ankle-length black coat for his friend's funeral, as well as a broad-brimmed black hat, a so-called slouch hat of the kind that has recently come back into fashion, especially among provincial actors. Of course we can't judge people by their clothes, I thought—that's a mistake I've never made—but at first everything about Joana's companion, with whom she's said to have lived for eight years, struck me as revolting—the way he spoke, what he said, the way he walked, and above all the way he ate his food in the *Iron Hand*. I was shattered to discover that Joana had in the end landed up with someone so *seedy*, who, after a spell as an actor at a small theater in the Josefstadt, had become a commercial traveler, hawking cheap earrings manufactured in Hong Kong; even for a commercial traveler he made a shabby impression, reminding me rather of a market trader—and the humblest kind

of market trader at that. The way he pronounced the words
potato salad to the waitress in the *Iron Hand* almost made
me want to vomit, I thought, sitting in the wing chair and
watching the guests in the music room. They somehow
seemed like figures on a distant stage; it was rather like
watching a moving photograph through the haze of cigarette smoke that had formed as a result of everyone's smoking. The Auersbergers suddenly announced they would
hold supper only for another quarter of an hour. We'll
wait till *half past twelve at the latest,* the hostess said to
the writer Jeannie Billroth, to whom she had been talking
for some time, naturally about Joana. This woman, who
was now fat and gross and ugly, fancied herself as the
Viennese Virginia Woolf, though everything she wrote was
the most dreadful kitsch, and in her novels and short stories
she never rose above a kind of loquacious, convoluted
sentimentality. This woman, who had come to the Gentzgasse in a black home-knitted woolen dress, had also been
a friend of Joana's. She lived in the Second District, not
far from the Praterhauptallee, and had for years actually
imagined herself to be *Austria's greatest writer, its greatest
literary artist.* This evening—or rather night—in the Gentzgasse she had no compunction in telling Auersberger's wife
that in her latest novel she had *gone a step further* than
Virginia Woolf (I was able to hear her say this because
I have such acute hearing, especially at night). Her new
book far surpassed *The Waves,* she said, whereupon she
lit a cigarette and crossed her legs. She said she intended
to go and see *The Wild Duck* again. In Ibsen there's so
much beneath the surface, she remarked to Auersberger's
wife. She had been unable to buy a copy of the play at
any Viennese bookshop; not one bookshop in the city
center had *The Wild Duck* in stock, she said—she had

not even managed to find a paperback edition. But naturally she knew *The Wild Duck*; she loved Ibsen, especially *Peer Gynt*, she said, speaking through a smoke screen of her own making. She was a heavy smoker and consequently had a raucous voice, and her face was bloated from overindulgence in white wine. In the days when I had close ties with the Auersbergers I used to spend a good deal of time with Jeannie Billroth—far too much time, as I now realize—in her municipal apartment, where she lived for more than ten years with a chemist called Ernstl, who never got around to marrying her—or whom she never got around to marrying. Ernstl earned the money, and Jeannie contributed her reputation, attracting artists and pseudo-artists, scientists and pseudo-scientists, and—as Joana used to say—*bringing color into their drab municipal apartment* with its utterly petit bourgeois atmosphere. Jeannie herself was nothing if not petit bourgeois and had become set in her petit bourgeois ways over the years, I thought as I sat in the wing chair. After the death of my friend Josef Maria, who hanged himself just as Joana did later, and who edited Austria's first official *literary magazine*, entitled *Literature in Our Time*, in the early fifties, Jeannie took over the editorship, with the result that the magazine became unreadable. It became a thoroughly dreary publication, utterly worthless and witless, subsidized by our dreadful, disgusting and benighted state, and carrying only the most fatuous and inane contributions, pride of place being given time and again to poems by Jeannie Billroth herself, who was convinced that she was not only the successor, even the surpasser, of Virginia Woolf, but also a *direct successor and surpasser of Annette von Droste-Hülshoff*, Germany's greatest woman poet. She fancied she wrote *the best poetry in Austria*, but she actually wrote

unrelievedly bad poetry, in which neither the sentiments
nor the ideas had the slightest literary merit. For fifteen
years she edited this pedestrian periodical, until she was
finally bought out with the promise of a life pension. But
this did nothing to improve its quality, I thought: on the
contrary, the present editor is if anything even more stupid
and inept than Jeannie. It was unfortunate, I thought,
sitting in the wing chair, that I had chosen that particular
day, March 14, to go to the Graben, intending to buy
myself a tie in the Kohlmarkt or the Naglergasse—I've always bought my ties in the Kohlmarkt and the Naglergasse—only to fall into the clutches of the Auersbergers.
In all probability they wouldn't have spoken to me, I now
reflected, had they not had the pretext of telling me about
Joana's death, and I'd never have accepted their supper
invitation had I not been *thrown off balance*, as it were,
by Joana's death. Naturally I had not recognized the woman
from the general store in Kilb when she telephoned; I did
not recognize her voice, having last heard it twenty years
before at Kilb, when I had taken her and Joana to the *Iron
Hand*, for a meal of cold sausage and salad—for a few
hours' relaxation and amusement, in other words—as I
now recalled distinctly, sitting in the wing chair. She had
told me over the telephone that Joana must have hanged
herself between three and four in the morning. This was
the conclusion reached by the doctor, who had cut down
the body with his own hands from a beam over the door
of the entrance hall. Country doctors aren't squeamish, I
thought. I had seen this doctor, a childhood friend of Joana's,
at the cemetery. The funeral was a grotesque affair. I had
taken the train to St. Pölten and then changed onto the
Maria Zell branch, arriving at Kilb at half past ten. In
order to arrive by ten thirty (the funeral was scheduled

for one thirty) I had to be at the Vienna West Station by half past seven. I had turned down various offers from friends to drive me there. I attach the greatest importance to being independent, and there is hardly anything I hate more than accepting lifts from other people and so being at their mercy for good or ill. I had clear recollections of the landscape between St. Pölten and Kilb, and even on this sad occasion it did not disappoint me. During the journey through the hills of Lower Austria I naturally recalled my earlier visits to Joana, most of which I had made either with her husband, the tapestry artist, or with the Auersbergers. But I had often gone there alone too, when I happened to be over from England; I recalled these cross-country journeys to Kilb with the utmost pleasure. Wherever I travel I prefer to be alone, just as I prefer to be alone when I am out *walking*. Yet it had always been a great joy to know that at the end of the journey to Kilb I would find Joana in her parents' little one-story house. I always made these journeys in the spring or the fall, never in summer and never in winter. Country girls, as soon as they are capable of making plans, set their sights on Vienna, the big city, I thought as I sat in the wing chair, and that hasn't changed. Joana had to go to Vienna, as she wanted at all costs to make a *career* for herself. She just couldn't wait for the day when she would board the Vienna train for good, so to speak. But Vienna brought her more heartache than happiness, I thought, sitting in the wing chair. Young people set off for the capital and come to grief, in the truest sense of the word, in the very place where they have placed all their hopes, thanks to the appalling society they find there, as well as to their own natures, which are generally no match for this canni-balistic city. After all, Auersberger too had set his heart on making a career in Vienna, yet he'd made no more of a career there than Joana; all this time he's been chasing after a career that has so far eluded him, I reflected in the wing chair. He made life too easy for himself, I thought, sitting in the wing chair, and so did Joana: when it comes to making a career in the big city things don't just happen by themselves, and in Vienna they're even less likely to happen by themselves than they are elsewhere. The mistake they both made, I now reflected in the wing chair, was to think that Vienna would come to their aid, that it would grab them under the arms, so to speak, and stop them from falling. But the city doesn't grab anyone under the arms: on the contrary, it constantly seeks to fend off the unfortunate people who repair to it in search of a career, to destroy them and annihilate them. It destroyed and annihilated not only Joana, but Auersberger too, who once believed that in Vienna he would be able to develop into an important composer, a composer of international importance, though to tell the truth he was not only unable to develop in Vienna—he was utterly ruined by the city. The genius he brought with him from Styria, of which there were unmistakable signs some thirty years ago, I now reflected, soon wasted away in Vienna; first it suffered a body blow, and then it became stunted, like countless other geniuses before it, especially musical geniuses. In Vienna he inevitably succumbed to atrophy and dwindled into a so-called *successor of Webern*, and he has remained a *successor of Webern* ever since. And Joana dreamed all her life of making a career for herself as a ballerina at the Opera, and finally of becoming a famous actress at the Burgtheater, yet all her life she remained a dilettante both as a dancer and as an actress, a movement therapist, so to speak, giving private lessons in deportment. It's now twenty-five years,

I thought, since I used to write playlets for her, which she would then perform for me during the afternoons and evenings we spent in her high-rise in the Simmeringer Hauptstrasse, and which we would record on tape for all time, as it were—dozens of pieces for two voices, in which she would try to prove how gifted she was and I would try to show off my literary and histrionic talents. These plays have been lost; they were quite devoid of literary merit, but for years they kept Joana and me alive, I now thought, sitting in the wing chair. For years I would set out, every two or three days, from my apartment in the Eighteenth District and catch the No. 71 tram out to the Simmeringer Hauptstrasse, call at Dittrich's liquor store opposite Joana's high-rise and buy three or four two-liter bottles of the cheapest white wine, then take the elevator to Joana's apartment on the eleventh floor. As we drank we would practice the *total theatrical art*, which comprises both acting and play writing, more or less relying on the wine to sustain us, until we were quite exhausted. When we were no longer capable of performing, we would play back the recordings we had made and get high on them until well into the night, in fact until morning came. My relationship with Joana, I reflected in the wing chair, played an important part in my own development. It was Joana who brought me back to the theater, which I had abandoned after passing out of the Academy. I'd left the Academy with my certificate, I now recalled, thinking as I went down the staircase that I was now through with theater studies and that I wanted nothing more to do with the theater for the rest of my life. I actually shunned the theater for years, until Auersberger introduced me to Joana. Then the moment I met her she suggested the idea of writing playlets for her—short dramatic sketches, in other words. She had the perfect voice. It was not *the way she looked* that fascinated me, but *the way she spoke*. And in fact it was my acquaintance with her, which eventually developed into a friendship, that quite simply brought me back into contact with art and things artistic, after I had been averse to them for so long. For me Joana, and everything about her, represented the theater. Besides, her husband painted, and this also fascinated me, right from the beginning, I recalled in the wing chair. Under the right circumstances she could probably have become one of the greatest artists, either as a dancer or as an actress, I thought as I sat in the wing chair, had she not met her artistic husband, Fritz, the painter turned tapestry artist, and had she not given in when she came up against the first serious obstacles to her ambition. On the other hand those of her fellow students from the Reinhardt Seminar who actually went on to act at the Theater in the Josefstadt or the Burgtheater, although they are now famous, succeeded only in becoming rather ridiculous and basically futile theatrical figures, who appear in perhaps one Shakespeare play, one Nestroy play and one Grillparzer play a year and are assuredly a thousand times more stupid than Joana ever was. This evening's gathering, though planned as an *artistic dinner* in honor of the actor, is in fact only a requiem for Joana, I said to myself: the smell of that afternoon's funeral was suddenly present in the Gentzgasse, the smell of the cemetery at Kilb was here in the Auersbergers' apartment. This so-called *artistic dinner* is really a funeral feast, I thought, and at once it occurred to me that to my certain knowledge the actor we were waiting for was the only supper guest who had *not* known Joana. The date for this *artistic dinner* had already been agreed, first of all with the actor from the Burgtheater, before

Joana killed herself; the Auersbergers had said more than once that it was intended as a belated celebration of the premiere of *The Wild Duck*, which had just opened at the Burgtheater. Joana's death had intervened in their dinner arrangements; they told the guests that it was a dinner in honor of the actor, but then intimated—though not in so many words—that it was in memory of Joana. The actor's convinced that this *artistic dinner* is being given for him, and that's enough to satisfy the Auersbergers, though of course they are giving it more for Joana, since it's taking place on the day of her funeral, I thought, sitting in the wing chair. At that moment I recalled that on the previous day I too had intended to read *The Wild Duck*, in order to be able to keep up with the actor, thinking that I needed only to open my bookcase and get out the text. But I was wrong: I had no copy of *The Wild Duck*, though I had been convinced that I had one. I'm bound to have a copy of the play, I had thought as I opened my bookcase. I've read it several times during the course of my life, I had thought, and I can even remember what the editions look like. But I really did not have a copy, and so, like Jeannie Billroth, I decided to buy myself one in town, but was unable to find one. However, sitting in the wing chair, I remembered that one of the characters in the play was called *Old Ekdal*, and that he had a son, *Young Ekdal*, who was a photographer. And I remembered that the first act took place at the home of a manufacturer called Werle. Ekdal has a studio in the attic, I reminded myself; gradually it all came back, and so I no longer had to exert my memory. Can this production of *The Wild Duck* be any good, I wondered, sitting in the wing chair, *if it's being put on by actors from the Burgtheater*? And again I thought of the *Iron Hand*, where I had taken the woman from the general store, who was dressed all in black, after arriving at Kilb. I entered the store only for a moment, to let her know that I had arrived. She immediately put on a black coat and accompanied me to the *Iron Hand*, the operations room, so to speak, for Joana's funeral. We both ordered a small goulash and waited for Joana's companion to arrive. He arrived at about half past eleven and joined us at our table. When people are dressed in black they appear un-usually pale, and this companion of Joana's (the woman from the general store insisted on calling her *Elfriede*) was so pale that he looked as though he were about to vomit at any moment. He actually did feel like vomiting when he approached our table, as he had come straight from the mortuary chapel next to the church, where he said he had been shattered by what they had shown him: without any prior warning he had had to *endure the sight* of Joana's body in a plastic bag. It appeared that the mortician, who as usual was the local carpenter, had been given no precise instructions about how the deceased was to be buried and had simply put Joana's body in a plastic bag pending the arrival of her companion that morning—this being the cheapest way of dealing with it—and left it on a trestle support in the mortuary chapel. He told us that on seeing the plastic bag he had felt sick and instructed the sexton to cover the body in a shroud and put it in a beech coffin; these instructions had been carried out with his assistance. While we all ate our goulash he told us that he simply could not describe what it had been like to pull Joana's body out of the plastic bag and cover it with a shroud—it had all been so *gruesome*. Finally he had chosen the most expensive coffin the carpenter had in stock.

Having eaten half his goulash he went out into the corridor to wash his hands; when he returned I could see tears in his eyes. There were no relatives left, he said; they'd all *died on her* long ago, as he put it, and so all the funeral arrangements *fell to him*. He had expected that the woman from the general store would have seen to Joana's body and everything arising from her suicide, but at this she shook her head and said that she could not have left her shop even for an hour and had assumed that he had all the arrangements in hand. Be that as it may, Joana's companion ate his goulash so quickly that he had already finished it when I was only halfway through mine. He accidentally splashed some of the gravy on his white starched shirt—or rather on his white starched shirtfront, for I noticed that he was not wearing a shirt, only a shirtfront over a woolen undervest, I recalled in the wing chair. This starched shirtfront spotted with gravy more or less confirms my impression that Joana's companion was completely down and out, I thought as I sat in the wing chair. Having finished his goulash he waited impatiently for us to finish ours, but neither of us could eat any faster. In the end I left nearly half of mine, but the woman from the general store managed to force down the rest of hers. If there's nobody around to pay the expenses, said Joana's companion, they simply put the body in a plastic bag. And then he said that there had been a frightful *stench* in the mortuary chapel. Looking out of the window of the inn, I saw several cars go past with people I knew in them; they had clearly come to Kilb for the funeral and were making for the cemetery. What a good thing I've brought my English umbrella with me, I thought, when it began to rain. The street outside grew dark, and the

inn parlor even darker. Jeannie Billroth, the writer, walked
past with her retinue, all of them young people under
twenty. It was actually *in the high-rise* that I last saw Joana,
I now recalled saying to myself in the *Iron Hand*; her face
was bloated and her legs swollen. She spoke in what anybody would have described as a *drunken voice*. Over the
bed hung one of her husband's tapestries, thick with dust,
a reminder of the fact that she had once been happy with
this man. The apartment was full of dirty laundry and
stank abominably. The tape recorder by the bed, where
I could see she spent virtually the whole day, was out of
order. On the floor were dozens of empty white wine
bottles, some standing, some knocked over. I wanted to
hear a particular tape we had made four or five years
before this surprise visit of mine, a tape of a sketch in which
I had played a king and Joana a princess, but the tape
was nowhere to be found. Even if we had found it there
would have been no point, as the tape recorder was
broken. *Naturally you were a naked princess*, I said to
Joana as she lay in bed. *And you were a naked king*, she
replied. She tried to laugh, but could not. There was nothing touching about this last visit of mine, nothing sentimental, I thought, sitting in the wing chair—I found it
simply nauseating. There were signs of a companion about
the apartment—a pack of cigarettes here, an old tie there,
a dirty sock, and so on. She told me several times that I
had let her down. She could hardly sit up in bed; she tried
several times, but each time she fell back. *You let me down,
you let me down*, she kept on saying. For the last few
years, she said, she had lived by selling off the tapestries
her husband had left behind. She had not heard from Fritz.
And she had not heard from the others either—she meant

the artistic crowd—she had heard *nothing from any of them*. She asked me to go down to Dittrich's and get two two-liter bottles of white wine. *Go on!* she said, just as she always had, *Go on! Go on!* She ordered me down to the liquor store, and I obeyed, just as I had done twenty or twenty-five years before. When I got back I put the two bottles by the bed and took my leave. There would have been no point in having any further conversation with her, I told myself as I sat in the wing chair. At the time I thought she was finished, yet she went on living for several years, and that was what amazed me most. I can truthfully say that until I learned of her death I had assumed that she must have been dead for years. Not having seen her or heard from her for so many years, I had simply forgotten about her, I thought, sitting in the wing chair. The truth is that at times we are so close to certain people that we believe there is a lifelong bond between us, and then suddenly they vanish from our memory overnight, I thought as I sat in the wing chair. It's the way with actors, I told myself, sitting in the Auersbergers' wing chair, that they don't dine much before midnight, and those who keep company with actors have to pay for this dreadful habit of theirs. If we go to a restaurant with actors the soup is never served until half past eleven at the earliest, and the coffee stage isn't reached until about half past one. *The Wild Duck* is a relatively short play, I told myself, but then it takes at least half an hour to get from the Burgtheater to the Gentzgasse, and after the performance the actors have to take their curtain calls—and since *The Wild Duck* is such a great success, there'll have been fairly prolonged applause—so it'll be at least half an hour before the actors have taken off their makeup. So if the performance finished at ten thirty it'll take the actor, who after all is the person for whom this *artistic dinner* is being given, at least until twelve thirty to get to the Gentzgasse. The Auersbergers invited their guests for half past ten— that's monstrous, I told myself as I sat in the wing chair: they must have known that *The Wild Duck* went on till ten thirty and that consequently their Ekdal couldn't be in the Gentzgasse before half past twelve. If I'd thought carefully about when this *artistic dinner* was actually going to start, I certainly wouldn't have come, I thought. I go to the Graben to look for a tie, which naturally I don't find, I thought, and at the most inauspicious moment I run into the Auersbergers. It's as though time had stood still, I thought: all the guests at this *artistic dinner* are people who were their closest and most intimate friends thirty years ago, back in the fifties. Clearly none of these friends had ever severed their relations with the Auersbergers; throughout the twenty or thirty years in which I had had no contact with the Auersbergers, all these people had kept up with them, as they say. I suddenly felt like a deserter, a traitor. It's as though I'd betrayed the Auersbergers and everything I associate with them, I thought, and the same thought must have occurred to the Auersbergers and their guests too. But that did not worry me— quite the contrary, for even now, sitting in their wing chair in their apartment, I found the Auersbergers utterly repugnant, and their guests equally so; indeed I hated all of them, because they were in every way the exact *opposite* of myself. And now, as I tried to sit it out in the Auersbergers' apartment, anesthetized by a few glasses of champagne, I felt that my dislike of them had in fact always amounted to hatred, hatred of everything to do with them. We may be on terms of the most intimate friendship with people and believe that our friendship will last all our lives, and then one day we think we've been let down by these people whom we've always respected, admired, even loved more than all others, and consequently we hate and despise them and want nothing more to do with them, I thought as I sat in the wing chair; not wanting to spend the rest of our lives pursuing them with our hatred as we previously pursued them with our love and affection, we quite simply erase them from our memories. In fact I succeeded in evading the Auersbergers for more than two decades and avoiding any risk of meeting them, having devised a deliberate strategy for avoiding any further contact *with these monsters*, as I could not help calling them privately, and so the fact that I had evaded them for over twenty years was in no way fortuitous, I thought, sitting in the wing chair. Joana's suicide alone is to blame for the fact that, in spite of everything, I quite suddenly ran into them in the Graben. Their abrupt invitation to their dinner in honor of the *Wild Duck artist* and my equally abrupt acceptance were a classic illustration of the irrational way one reacts under stress. After all, even though I'd accepted the invitation, I didn't have to act upon it, especially as I've never been punctilious about keeping my promises to visit people, I thought. In fact during the whole of the interval between being invited to this *artistic dinner* and the dinner itself I had kept on wondering whether I would really go to it. At one moment I thought I would, at another I thought I wouldn't; now I told myself I'd go, now I told myself I wouldn't go. I'll go, I won't go—this word game went on in my head day after day, almost driving me insane, and even this evening, shortly before I finally set off for the Gentzgasse, I still wasn't sure whether I would go to the Gentzgasse. Only a few minutes before I finally decided to go I said to myself, Since you've just seen all over again, at the funeral in Kilb, that the Auersbergers are as repulsive as ever, you naturally *won't* go. The Auersbergers are repulsive people; it was they who betrayed you, not you who betrayed them, I kept thinking as I tried to freshen up in the bathroom, running ice-cold water over my wrists and at one stage trying to cool my face by holding it under the tap. Over the past twenty years they've run you down and denigrated you wherever they could, perverting the truth about everything connected with you and taking every opportunity to assassinate your character, I thought; they've told stories about you that aren't true, they've spread lies about you, vicious lies, more and more lies, hundreds and thousands of lies in the last twenty years, telling everybody that it was *you* who exploited *them* at Maria Zaal, not *they* who exploited *you*, that it was *you* who behaved outrageously, not they, that it was *you* who defamed *them*, not they who defamed you, that *you* were the traitor, and so on. I took into account all the reasons for not visiting them; I could find none in favor of doing so after being out of contact for twenty years, yet finally, despite my repugnance, despite the immense hatred I bore them, I made up my mind that I would visit them, and so I slipped on my coat and set out for the Gentzgasse. I've come to the Gentzgasse, I told myself, sitting in the wing chair, even though it's the last thing I wanted to do. Everything was against my coming to the Gentzgasse, everything was against such a ludicrous *artistic dinner*, yet now I'm here. *On the way to the Gentzgasse I kept saying to myself, I'm against this visit, I'm against the Auersbergers, I'm against all the people who are going to be there, I hate them, I hate all of them. And yet I kept on walking and finally rang the bell of their apartment.* Everything was against my making an appearance in the

Gentzgasse and yet I've made it, I said to myself as I sat in the wing chair. And again it occurred to me that I would have done better to read my Gogol and my Pascal and my Montaigne, or to play Schönberg or Satie, or just to take a walk through the streets of Vienna. And in fact the Auersbergers were even more surprised at my appearing in the Gentzgasse than I was myself, I thought. I could tell this from the way Auersberger's wife received me, and even more clearly from the way Auersberger himself received me. You shouldn't have come to the Gentzgasse, I told myself the moment I found myself facing her. It's an act of insanity, I told myself as I held out my hand to him. He didn't shake it—whether this was because he was drunk or because he was being abominably rude I can't say, I thought, sitting in the wing chair. They issued their invitation in the Graben in the belief that I wouldn't come under any circumstances, I thought, sitting in the wing chair; perhaps they themselves didn't really know why they invited me to their dinner, immediately referring to it as an *artistic dinner*—which was a fatal mistake, I thought, as it made them seem ridiculous. But the Auersbergers could have refrained from speaking to me in the Graben, I thought; they could have ignored me, as they had done for decades, just as I had ignored them for decades, I thought, sitting in the wing chair. Joana's to blame for this invitation, I thought, she's the cause of my irrational behavior, the dead woman has this distasteful *contretemps* on her conscience. Yet at the same time I thought how nonsensical such an idea was, but it kept coming back—again and again I had this non-sensical notion that the dead Joana was to blame for that *irrational reaction in the Graben*, which finally led to my coming to the Gentzgasse, against my natural inclinations, to take part in this *artistic dinner*. It was because of Joana's death that as soon as the Auersbergers saw me in the Graben they canceled the past twenty years, during which we had had absolutely no contact with one another, and issued their invitation, and for the selfsame reason I accepted it. And then of course they added that they had *invited the Burgtheater actor*, who was *enjoying such a triumph in The Wild Duck*, as Auersberger's wife put it, and I said I would come. Never in the last ten or fifteen years have I accepted an invitation to a dinner at which an actor was to be one of the guests, I thought as I sat in the wing chair, never have I gone anywhere where an actor was going to be present, and then suddenly I'm told that an actor is coming to dinner —an actor from the Burgtheater at that, and what's more to a dinner party at the Auersbergers' apartment in the Gentzgasse—and I go along. There was no point now in clapping my hand to my forehead. Actually I'm doing nothing to hide the revulsion I feel for all these people, and for the Auersbergers themselves, I told myself as I sat in the wing chair; on the contrary they can all sense that I loathe and detest them. They can't just see that I hate them—they can hear it too. Conversely I had the impression that all these people were hostile to me; from what I saw of them and in everything I heard them say, I sensed their aversion, even their hatred. The Auersbergers hated me; they realized that I was the blemish they had wished on their dinner party by being so thoughtless as to invite me; they were dreading the moment when the actor would enter the apartment and they would ask us all to take our places at table and begin the meal. They saw that I was the observer, the repulsive person who had made himself comfortable in the wing chair and was playing his disgusting observation game in the semidarkness of the anteroom, more or less *taking the guests apart*, as they say. They had always found it offensive that I should seize every opportunity of quite unscrupulously taking them apart, but in mitigation, I told myself as I sat in the wing chair, I could always plead that I took myself apart much more often than anybody else, never sparing myself, always dissecting myself *into all my component parts*, as they would say, with equal nonchalance, equal viciousness, and equal ruthlessness. In the end there was always much less left of me than there was of them, I told myself. I had one consolation: I was not the only one to curse the fact that I had come to the Gentzgasse, that I had been guilty of such imbecility and weakness of character—the Auersbergers too were cursing themselves for inviting me. But I was there, and nothing could be done about it. Thirty years ago I used to share their apartment with them, going in and out of it as though it were my own home, I thought as I sat in the wing chair observing what was happening in the music room, which was so brightly lit that nothing could escape me, while I remained in the dark all the time, occupying what was without doubt the most favorable position I could possibly occupy in this disagreeable situation. I had known all the guests at this *artistic dinner*, as I had known the Auersbergers themselves, virtually for decades, except for the young people; among these were two young writers, but they did not interest me: I did not know them and so had no reason whatever to concern myself with them, except to observe them. I did not feel the slightest urge to go over and talk to them, to challenge them to a conversation or an argument. I was probably too tired, for I had been completely exhausted by the strain of the funeral, by what I had gone through in Kilb for Joana's sake, I thought, above all the dreadful scenes *after* the funeral, which were so incredible that I shall only gradually be able to take them in; I still did not have the necessary mental clarity to comprehend them, and I thought I would need a thorough sleep before I could even begin. Sitting in the wing chair I was already starting to think that when I got home I would go straight to bed and not get up for the whole of the following day and the following night, perhaps even the next day and the next night too—so exhausted, so *worn out* did I feel as I sat in the wing chair. We imagine we are twenty and act accordingly, yet in fact we are over fifty and completely exhausted, I thought; we treat ourselves like twenty-year-olds and ruin ourselves, and we treat everybody else as though we were all still twenty, even though we're fifty and can't stand the pace any longer; we forget that we have a medical condition, more than one in fact, a number of medical conditions, a number of so-called *fatal diseases*, but we ignore them for as long as we can and don't take them seriously, though they're there all the time and ultimately kill us. We treat ourselves as though we still had the strength we had thirty years ago, whereas in fact we don't have a fraction of our former strength, not even a fraction, I thought, sitting in the wing chair. Thirty years ago I would think nothing of staying up for two or three nights on end, drinking virtually non-stop, not caring what I drank, and performing like an *entertainment machine*, playing the fool for several nights—round the clock, as they say—for all sorts of people, all of them friends, without doing myself the slightest harm. For years, as it now seems, I never got home before three or four in the morning; I would go to bed with the dawn chorus, yet it didn't do me the slightest harm. For years I would turn up at the *Apostelkeller* or some other dive in the city around eleven in the evening and not leave before three or four in the morning, having used up every possible drop of energy, I may say, with the utmost ruthlessness, though it was a ruthlessness which at that time was second nature to me and, as it now seems, did me no harm at all. And I spent countless nights talking and drinking with Joana, I thought as I sat in the wing chair. I had no money or possessions of any kind, yet the truth is that for years I whiled away the nights talking, drinking and dancing with Joana and her husband, with Jeannie Billroth, and above all with the Auersbergers. In those days I had all the energy a young man could possibly have, and I had no scruples about letting myself be supported by anyone better off than myself, I recalled in the wing chair. I never had a penny in my pocket, yet I could afford whatever I wanted, I thought, sitting in the wing chair and observing the guests in the music room. And for years I would go out every day to the Simmeringer Hauptstrasse in the late afternoon to spend the night with Joana, calling at Dittrich's on the way to pick up the wine, and then return in the early morning, either catching the No. 71 or walking back to Währing along the Simmeringer Hauptstrasse, down the Rennweg, and across the Schwarzenbergerplatz. In those days, I recalled, horse-drawn carts could still be seen parked at night in front of the dairies, and it was still possible to walk down the middle of the Rennweg, cut across the Schwarzenbergerplatz, and walk along the deserted Ring without being afraid of being run over. I seldom met another soul, and if I did it was sure to be one of my own kind—another late-night reveler—and it was a rarity to see a car cruising through the streets at that hour. Never in my life have I sung so many Italian arias as I did in those days as I walked from the Simmeringer Hauptstrasse to the

Rennweg, then across the Schwarzenbergerplatz and back to Währing, I thought as I sat in the wing chair. At that time I had the strength to walk *and* sing; now I'm not even strong enough to *walk and talk*—that's the difference. Thirty years ago I thought nothing of a ten-mile walk home at night, I recalled in the wing chair, *singing all the way in my youthful enthusiasm for Mozart and Verdi and giving vent to my intoxication.* It's thirty years, I thought, since I made operatic history in this way—thirty years. The truth is, I thought, sitting in the wing chair, that my life would have taken a different course had it not been for Joana; perhaps I'd have pursued a diametrically opposed course had I not met Auersberger. For my encounter with Auersberger meant essentially a return to things artistic, on which I had turned my back completely—and definitively, as I then believed—after leaving the Mozarteum. At that time, after passing out of the Mozarteum, I suddenly wanted nothing more to do with the supposedly artistic, having opted firmly for the opposite of what I would call *the artistic*, but then my meeting with Auersberger, I recalled in the wing chair, caused me once more to do a complete about-turn. And then I met Joana, I recalled, who was the quintessence of everything artistic. It was for the artistic, not for art, that I opted thirty-five years ago—only *the artistic*, I thought as I sat in the wing chair, *though I had no idea what that was.* I opted for *the artistic*, though I didn't know what form it would take. I quite simply opted for Auersberger, for Auersberger as he was then, thirty-five or thirty-four years ago, and as he still was thirty-three years ago—for *the artistic Auersberger*. And for Joana, the quintessentially *artistic Joana*. And for Vienna. And for the artistic world, I thought, sitting in the wing chair. I owe it to Auersberger that I executed an about-turn and returned to the artistic world, I thought, sitting in the wing chair, and above all I owe it to Joana—to everything that was connected with Auersberger and Joana thirty-five years ago, and was still connected with them thirty-two years ago—that's the truth, I thought, sitting in the wing chair. Several times I repeated to myself the words *the artistic world* and *the artistic life*. I actually spoke them out loud, in such a way that people in the music room were bound to hear them—as indeed they did, for all their heads suddenly turned in my direction, from the music room to the anteroom—though they could not actually see me—on hearing me repeating the words *the artistic life* and *the artistic world*. I recalled what the notions *artistic world* and *artistic life* had meant to me then, and still meant to me today—more or less *everything*, I now thought, sitting in the wing chair, and I thought how tasteless it was for the Auersbergers to call this dinner of theirs—or rather this supper—an *artistic dinner*. How low they've sunk, I thought as I sat in the wing chair—these people who as far as I can see have been artistically, intellectually and spiritually bankrupt for decades. But to all these people in the music room, hearing me utter the words *artistic world* and *artistic life*, it was of course as though I had said *artistic dinner* just as the Auersbergers might have done, and apart from being so audible they struck nobody as in any way unusual—nobody realized what they meant to me. At one time, of course, all these people had actually been artists, or at least possessed *artistic talents*, I thought, sitting in the wing chair, but now they were just so much *artistic riffraff*, having about as much to do with art and the artistic as this dinner party of the

Auersbergers'. All these people, who were once real artists, or at least in some way artistic, I thought as I sat in the wing chair, are now nothing but shams, husks of their former selves: I have only to listen to what they say, I have only to look at them, I have only to come into contact with their products, to feel exactly the same way about them as I feel about this supper party, this tasteless *artistic dinner*. To think what has happened to all these people over the past thirty years, I thought, to think what they've made of themselves in these thirty years! And what I've made of myself in these thirty years! It's unrelievedly depressing to see what they've made of themselves, what I've made of myself. All these people have contrived to turn conditions and circumstances that were once happy into something utterly depressing, I thought, sitting in the wing chair; they've managed to make everything depressing, to transform all the happiness they once had into utter depression, just as I have. For there's no doubt that thirty or even twenty years ago all these people were happy, but now they're unutterably depressing, every bit as depressing and unhappy as I am myself, I thought as I sat in the wing chair. They've transformed sheer happiness into sheer misery, I thought, sitting in the wing chair, unalloyed hope into unrelieved hopelessness. For what I saw when I looked into the music room was a scene of unmitigated hopelessness, both human and artistic, I thought, sitting in the wing chair—that's the truth. All these people had come to Vienna in the fifties, thirty years earlier, some of them forty years earlier, hoping they would go far, as they say, but the farthest they *actually* went in Vienna was to become tolerably successful provincial artists, and the question is whether they would have gone any farther in any other so-called big city—*they* probably wouldn't have gone very far anywhere, I thought. But when I reflect that they've got nowhere in Vienna, nowhere at all, I thought, I also realize that they're unaware of this, for they don't act as though they were aware of having got nowhere: on the contrary they behave as though they'd gone far in Vienna, as though every one of them had become something worthwhile; they think that all the hopes they placed in Vienna have been fulfilled, I thought, or at least most of the time they believe they've gone far—most of the time they believe fervently that they've become something worthwhile, although from my point of view they haven't become anything. Because they've made *a name* for themselves, won *a lot of prizes*, published a lot of books, and sold their pictures to a lot of museums, because they've had their books issued by the best publishing houses and their pictures hung in the best museums, because they've been awarded every possible prize that this appalling state has to offer and had every possible decoration pinned to their breasts, they believe they've become something, though in fact they've become nothing, I thought. They're all what are termed *well-known artists*, *celebrated artists*, who sit as senators in the so-called *Art Senate*; they call themselves professors and have chairs at our academies; they are invited by this or that college or university to speak at this or that symposium; they travel to Brussels or Paris or Rome, to the United States and Japan and the Soviet Union and China, where sooner or later they're invited to give lectures about themselves and open exhibitions of their pictures, and yet as I see it they haven't become anything. They've all quite simply failed to achieve *the highest*, and as I see it *only the highest* can bring real *satisfaction*, I thought. Auersberger's compositions don't go unperformed,

I thought, sitting in the wing chair; *Auersberger, the successor of Webern, hasn't failed to gain recognition,* I thought. On the contrary, not a moment passes without something of his being sung, without one of his compositions being performed by brass, woodwind, strings or percussion (he makes sure of that!)—now in Basel, now in Zürich, now in London, now in Klagenfurt—here a duet, there a trio, here a four-minute chorus, there a twelve-minute opera, here a three-minute cantata, there a one-second opera, a one-minute song, a two-minute or four-minute aria; sometimes he engages English performers, sometimes French or Italian; sometimes his work is performed by a Polish or Portuguese violinist, sometimes by a Chilean or Italian lady on the clarinet. Hardly has he arrived in one town than he's thinking about the next, our restless successor of Webern, it seems, our mincing, globe-trotting imitator of Webern and Grafen, our snobbish, musical dandy from the Styrian sticks. Just as Bruckner is unendurably monumental, so Webern is unendurably meager, yet the meagerness of Anton Webern is as nothing compared with the meagerness of Auersberger, whom I am bound to describe as the *almost noteless* composer, just as the mindless literary experts have dubbed Paul Celan the *almost wordless* poet. This Styrian imitator doesn't go unperformed, but thirty years ago, in the mid-fifties, he was already stuck in the Webern tradition; he's never written so much as three notes without making some composition or other out of them. What is missing in Auersberger's compositions, it seems to me, is Auersberger himself; his aphoristic music (which was how I described his derivative compositions in the fifties!) is nothing but an *unendurable copy* of Webern, who was himself, as I now realize, not the genius he was taken to be, but only a sudden—if brilliant—

access of debility in the history of music. In fact I feel heartily ashamed of myself as I sit in the Auersbergers' wing chair and reflect that Auersberger was never a genius, even though back in the fifties I was utterly convinced that he was: he was simply a pathetic little bourgeois with a certain talent, who gambled away his talent in his first few weeks in Vienna. Vienna is a terrible machine for the destruction of genius, I thought, sitting in the wing chair, an appalling recycling plant for the demolition of talent. All these people whom I was now observing through their sickening cigarette smoke came to Vienna thirty or thirty-five years ago, hoping to go far, only to have whatever genius or talent they possessed annihilated and killed off by the city, which kills off all the hundreds and thousands of geniuses or talents that are born in Austria every year. They may think they've gone far, but in reality they haven't gone anywhere, I thought as I sat in the wing chair, and the reason is that they were content to stay in Vienna: they didn't leave at the decisive moment and go abroad, like all those who did achieve something; those who stayed behind in Vienna became nonentities, whereas I can say without hesitation that all those who went abroad made something of themselves. Because they were satisfied with Vienna, they ended up as nonentities, unlike those who left Vienna at the decisive moment and went abroad, I thought, sitting in the wing chair. I will not speculate about what might have become of all these people in the music room, all these people who were waiting around for the artist to make his entrance and for the *artistic dinner* to begin, if they had left Vienna at the crucial moment in their lives. It took no more than a minor success, a favorable press review of her first novel, to make Jeannie Billroth stay in Vienna, no more than the sale of a couple of pictures to national museums to make Rehmden the painter stay in Vienna, no more than a few fulsome notices in the *Kurier* or the *Presse* to persuade some promising actress to stay in Vienna. The music room is full of people who stayed on in Vienna, I thought as I sat in the wing chair. And at the cemetery in Kilb those who followed Joana's coffin were almost exclusively people who had stayed on in Vienna, almost suffocating in the comfort of their petit bourgeois world. What a depressing effect the funeral at Kilb had on me, for this reason more than any other! I thought, watching these people from the wing chair. What depressed me was not so much the fact that Joana was being buried as that the only people who followed her coffin were artistic corpses, failures, Viennese failures, the living dead of the artistic world—writers, painters, dancers and hangers-on, artistic cadavers not yet quite dead, who looked utterly grotesque in the pelting rain. The sight was not so much sad as unappetizing, I thought. All through the ceremony I was obsessed by the spectacle of these repellent artistic nonentities trudging behind the coffin through the cemetery mud in their distasteful attitudes of mourning, I told myself as I sat in the wing chair. It was not so much the funeral that aroused my indignation as the demeanor of the mourners who had turned up from Vienna in their flashy cars. I became so agitated that I had to take several heart tablets, yet my agitation was brought on not by the dead Joana, but by the behavior of these arty people, these artistic shams, I thought, and it occurred to me that my own behavior at Kilb had probably been equally distasteful. The very fact that I had put on a black suit was distasteful, I now told myself; so was the way I had eaten my goulash in the *Iron Hand* and the way I had talked to Joana's companion, as though I were the only person who had really been close to Joana, the only one who had any claim on her. The more I thought about the funeral, the more I became aware of the distasteful aspects of my own behavior: no matter what circumstances came to mind, they were all equally distasteful. Finding the others distasteful, I naturally could not help finding myself distasteful too, I thought, and the more I thought about everything connected with the funeral, the more reprehensible my own conduct seemed to me. It had been distasteful to go to Kilb *alone*, despite the fact that several people had offered to drive me there, I thought, and it had been distasteful to talk to the woman from the general store, Joana's friend, as though *I* had been closest to her; it had been inconsiderate to monopolize her company, leaving her no time to attend to the other people who had come to the funeral, I thought. *I* had made myself *the star of the funeral*, I thought, and I now saw how monstrous this had been. I had downgraded Joana's companion and all the others at the funeral and at the same time upgraded myself—and that was contemptible. On the other hand I had believed at the time that I was behaving *properly*. During the funeral I had been unaware of incurring any guilt: only now, sitting in the wing chair, did I develop what might be called a sense of guilt with regard to my conduct at Kilb. The fact that Joana had killed herself did not make me feel any sadder in Kilb, I thought, sitting in the wing chair: it simply aroused my indignation against her friends, though I could not explain to myself why this should be. The truth is that I was not in the least shocked to get the telephone call from the owner of the general store, informing me that Joana had committed suicide; I *pretended* to be shocked, I now reflected, but in fact I wasn't—I was *curious, but not shocked.* I only *feigned* shock; I was merely curious and immediately wanted her to tell me everything about Joana's suicide. I displayed the most outrageous curiosity, and it was only now, sitting in the wing chair, that I felt shocked by this —by the fact that I had not been sad, but merely curious, and that I had forced more information out of the woman than she was willing to impart, for during our telephone conversation she showed a decency that was entirely lacking in me. Naturally Joana had become such a stranger to me and we had been out of touch for so many years, that the call from the woman at the general store, as I have said, could not possibly have come as a shock, nor could it cause me any immediate sadness; it produced merely curiosity, and this curiosity forced her to tell me everything about Joana's suicide there and then. I was interested not in the fact of her suicide, but in the circumstances. I was *sad*. I was *really saddened*, and it was in this mood of sadness that I walked into town—to the Graben, the Kärntnerstrasse and the Kohlmarkt, then to the *Bräunerhof* in the Spiegelgasse, where I glanced through the *Corriere*, *Le Monde*, the *Zürcher Zeitung* and the *Frankfurter Allgemeine Zeitung*, as I had been in the habit of doing for years. Then, sickened by the newspapers, I went back to the Graben to buy myself a tie, but instead of buying a tie I ran into the Auersbergers, to be told once again about Joana's suicide. By now I knew much more about it than they did, yet I pretended to know nothing. I put on such an act of bewilderment that the couple must have felt I was shocked by Joana's suicide, whereas in fact I was only *feigning* shock. I had actually felt saddened by Joana's suicide as I walked back and forth in the city, and then, quite suddenly and quite shamelessly, I pretended to the Auersbergers that I was shocked by it. And just as my shock was feigned, so too was my acceptance of the invitation to their *artistic dinner*, because the whole of my conduct toward the Auersbergers during our meeting in the Graben was pure dissembling. Sitting in the wing chair, I reflected that I had *pretended* to be shocked by Joana's suicide and pretended to accept the Auersbergers' invitation to their *artistic dinner*. When I accepted it I was only pretending, I now thought, yet in spite of this I had acted upon it. The idea is nothing short of grotesque, I thought, yet at the same time it amused me. Actually I've always dissembled with the Auersbergers, I thought, sitting in the wing chair, and here I am again, sitting in their wing chair and dissembling once more: I'm not really here in their apartment in the Gentzgasse, I'm only pretending to be in the Gentzgasse, only pretending to be in their apartment, I said to myself. I've always pretended to them about everything—I've pretended to everybody about everything. My whole life has been a pretense, I told myself in the wing chair—the life I live isn't real, it's a simulated life, a simulated existence. My whole life, my whole existence has always been *simulated*—my life has *always been pretense*, never reality, I told myself. And I pursued this idea to the point at which I finally *believed* it. I drew a deep breath and said to myself, in such a way that the people in the music room were bound to hear it: *You've always lived a life of pretense, not a real life—a simulated existence, not a genuine existence. Everything about you, everything you are, has always been pretense, never genuine, never real.* But I must put an end to this fantasizing lest I go mad, I thought, sitting in the wing chair, and so I took a large gulp of champagne. While I had been drinking champagne all the time, the people in the music room, as I could see, had been content with sherry and in the end simply with water, not wanting to get as recklessly drunk before supper, before the so-called *artistic dinner*, as Auersberger was already. *I* was not afraid of drinking too much, and so I went on drinking. But naturally I did not drink so recklessly that I became as drunk as the host. I continued to drink, but confined myself to one mouthful every ten or fifteen minutes—that is the truth. After all I was no longer twenty, but fifty-two—a fact that I never once forgot during this evening in the Gentzgasse. At Kilb all these *artistic people* had seemed grotesque. Their *artistic preoccupations* and their *artistic activity* made them seem somehow unnatural, at least to me: they had an *artificial way of walking*, an *artificial way of talking; everything* about them was artificial, whereas the cemetery itself seemed the most natural place in the world. When they bowed their heads they bowed them too low. When they stood up or sat down they did so *too soon* (or too late); when they started to sing they did so *too soon* (or too late). When they spoke the responses they spoke them *too soon* (or too late)—whereas the local people, of whom there was *a good turnout*, as they say, did everything naturally—they spoke naturally, sang naturally, walked naturally, stood up and sat down naturally, doing nothing too soon or too late or too quickly or too slowly. And whereas the artistic people from Vienna were grotesquely attired for the funeral, the local people were dressed with the utmost propriety, I reflected as I sat in the wing chair. The local people were in tune with the village and its cemetery, while the artistic folk from Vienna clashed with both. The metropolitan note struck by these Viennese mourners is out of keeping with this village cemetery, I had thought as I walked in the long cortege. Every one of these mourners from Vienna is a foreign body

in Kilb, I had thought as I followed the coffin, walking between the woman from the general store and Joana's unhappy companion, who coughed as though he had some
lung disease all the way from the church to the cemetery
(which must have been over a mile). The possibility that
he might have lung disease made me anxious, and whenever
he coughed I held my breath for fear of being infected,
until suddenly I reflected that I too had lung disease and
was probably more infectious than he was, whereupon I
began to cough even more than he did, and as soon as I
started coughing he stopped, as though realizing that *I* had
lung disease and might infect *him*, for as soon as I began
coughing he turned his face the other way and held a
paper tissue to his nose as he walked. The woman from
the general store wore a gray waterproof coat, the most
sensible garment I saw at the funeral, I thought as I sat in
the wing chair. In fact the local people were all sensibly
dressed, whereas all the people from Vienna got hopelessly
drenched, and those who had come in their ostentatious
fur coats, expecting the weather to be cold (though in
fact it was fairly warm), seemed grotesque and ludicrous;
moreover the rain at once made them look messy, trickling
down their fur coats like so much dirty gravy. Their
umbrellas were soon blown inside out, and some were
broken, by a fierce gust of wind that blew across the graves
from the mountains as the cortege reached the cemetery.
As always on such occasions, I recalled in the wing chair,
the village priest had delivered a totally inept address at
the graveside. All the same, times have changed, I remembered thinking as I stood at the graveside: *he was at least
delivering an address*—only ten or twelve years earlier
no priest would have delivered an address by a suicide's

grave anywhere in Austria. It was as primitive as all the other graveside addresses I have heard, and the voice of the priest, who seemed to have some kind of throat ailment, was so disagreeable and high-pitched that it hurt my ears to listen to it. Unfortunately, however, his address was also comprehensible and contained all the mendacity and hypocrisy the Catholic Church purveys on such occasions. Toward the end he recalled that he and Joana had both attended the village school and that he liked to remember her as the *nice local girl,* and referring to her years in Vienna he spoke of the *morass of the big city.* He had the face of a small town official, not a typical peasant face, but the kind of face we find ourselves looking at whenever we go into a country store and ask for a hammer or a hoe, a pair of rubber boots or a scouring cloth, I thought, sitting in the wing chair—a sly, distrustful face that we dare not look at for more than a few seconds. By attending this funeral, I thought as I sat in the wing chair, this whole artistic contingent from Vienna was subjecting itself to a Catholic ceremonial with which it was no longer familiar (if it ever had been) or had become unfamiliar over the years, as I had; having had no contact with this kind of Catholic ceremonial for decades, if for no other reason, I found it entirely hypocritical. The Viennese mourners pretended to know when to stand up and when not, what to sing, what prayers to say and when, yet like me they were completely at sea. Consequently they prayed and sang *mezza voce* in a way that nobody could understand, always sitting down and standing up a second later than the local people. This Viennese artistic contingent only mouthed their words, and so the effect they produced was merely theatrical, I thought, and so was the effect I produced—or failed to produce, as the case may be. During the funeral my mind was totally occupied with the contents of Joana's coffin and what they must look like. Throughout the ceremony my mind was taken up by this one abominable thought. After everything that Joana's companion had told us in the *Iron Hand* about his experience in the mortuary chapel, I could not expel this obscene thought from my mind during the whole of the funeral ceremony, however hard I tried, for in all truth I did not wish to think about such a thing—naturally not, I thought, sitting in the wing chair, and it occurred to me that what had prompted these speculations about the contents of the coffin was the complete lack of embarrassment shown by Joana's companion (whom the woman from the general store always addressed as *John*, though I did not yet know why) as he gave us his grisly account of his visit to the mortuary chapel and the transfer of Joana's body. John shouldn't have returned from the mortuary chapel and told us this story while we were eating our goulash, I thought, sitting in the wing chair; on the other hand I now admired him precisely for his lack of embarrassment and his obvious truthfulness, and I reflected that it would have been impossible for me or any of these artistic folk to give such an unembarrassed account of the transfer of the body. The mention of the *plastic bag* made me feel sick, and indeed John did not spare us any details of the proceedings in the mortuary chapel. Only an unartistic person like him would have been capable of giving such a grisly account without feeling embarrassed, yet at the same time without any appearance of indecency, for there seemed to be nothing indecent about what he said, whereas it would have seemed indecent had anyone

else said it. I reflected that it would have been indecent—
indeed it would have been base and contemptible—had I
given a similar account of the transfer of the body. John
remained silent throughout the funeral, whereas all the
others whispered to one another from time to time, I
thought. It had seemed strange to all who were present
that he should be the first to step up to the edge of the
grave, take a handful of earth from the shovel held out to
him by the sexton, and throw it onto the coffin lying far
below, though probably none of them could have said why
it seemed strange; in fact it was entirely logical for him to
do so, since Joana's former husband, the tapestry artist,
was not present and there were apparently no surviving
relatives. Standing by Joana's open grave he looked both
ugly and pathetic; the people watching him were profoundly disturbed by the sight, and I myself was revolted
by it, though privately (without expressing or in any way
indicating how I felt) I was prepared to think of him as
a *good man*. He's a *good man*, I said to myself, seeing him
standing like that beside Joana's grave; I do not know
what prompted this reaction, and it is not important. While
we were still at the graveside Auersberger's wife spoke
to me and asked me whether I would like to drive back
to Vienna with them, but I immediately refused with a
brusqueness which never fails to give offense whenever
I resort to it. I simply said *No*. Afterwards, in the *Iron
Hand*, most of the people from Vienna got together at a
long table; I had to sit there too, the Auersbergers having
more or less forced me to do so by addressing me in characteristic fashion in front of all the others and inviting me
to join them, in such a way that I was unable to refuse.
I would much rather have sat at the same table as Joana's

companion, the woman from the general store, and one or two other local people who had been childhood friends of Joana's. The Auersbergers forced me, by the *manner* of their invitation, to sit at their table, which was something I had been dreading throughout the funeral: I had no wish to spend even the shortest time with them *in Kilb*, since I was invited to their *artistic dinner* that same evening in the Gentzgasse. I pretended to be struck dumb by grief over Joana's suicide and did not say a word, while the Auersbergers and the others had a goulash like the one I had had before the funeral. I ordered myself a plate of sliced sausage and salad with extra onions; I also ate a couple of rolls, something I had never done before—simply out of nervousness. The Auersbergers talked incessantly about their *artistic dinner*, to which they had invited the actor, the Burgtheater actor, and they kept on saying how much this *tragedian* (as Auersberger's wife insisted on calling him) had impressed them in *The Wild Duck*. Auersberger's wife kept on wanting to tell us what role the actor had played in *The Wild Duck*, but she could not remember, until in the end *I* said *Ekdal*, whereupon, in a hysterical outburst, she shouted the name *Ekdal* across the room in a way that embarrassed everyone. She kept on shouting *Ekdal, Ekdal, Ekdal, right, Ekdal*, until her husband told her to calm down. Auersberger, little paunchy Auersberger, was of course drunk as usual. He had been drunk during the funeral service, I thought, sitting in the wing chair. He's been drunk almost continuously for as long as I've known him—it's a miracle that he's still alive; twice a year he goes to Kalksburg for a drying-out cure, I thought, and that's apparently enough to keep him alive. He had the same bloated face he had had twenty years earlier—hardly any wrinkles, the characteristic gelatinous gray complexion, the same glassy blue eyes as before, I thought. *Ekdal, Ekdal,* his wife kept screaming, though nobody in the room knew what she was screaming about. Finding her so repellent as she shouted out *Ekdal, Ekdal,* I became very rude and asked, *Which Ekdal? What do you mean—which Ekdal?* she asked. To which I replied, *Old Ekdal or Young Ekdal?* There was a pause, during which everyone stared at her; she saw that I was needling her—in the most despicable fashion, I am bound to admit—and without looking up from her goulash she said, *Old Ekdal.* At that point she really hated me, I thought, sitting in the wing chair. I could have slapped her face. Then her husband, who by now seemed totally drunk, suddenly pushed his goulash to the middle of the table and shouted toward the kitchen door, *This food's abominable!* He shouted these words in a voice of purest upstart viciousness. I had had the same goulash before the funeral and found it quite excellent, and all the others who had ordered goulash were of my opinion, not his. For as long as I have known him Auersberger has always found fault with the food served at any inn or restaurant, even the choicest. At least it was ill-mannered to make such a scene, especially at an excellent establishment like the *Iron Hand,* which I know to be generally well run, I thought, sitting in the wing chair. For as long as he's been married to his wife, who provides the financial support, Auersberger has always behaved atrociously in restaurants. Having yelled these words in the direction of the kitchen, he leaned back in his chair and stuck his tongue out at his wife. During the course of their marriage she had become so accustomed to her husband's tasteless foolery that she was not at all surprised when he stuck his tongue out at her. She merely lowered her head and tried to finish the goulash, for which he had wanted to destroy her appetite. Her manner of eating, while hardly the acme of refinement, was not inelegant, whereas her husband's had always been simply comic, I suddenly thought, sitting in the wing chair. This *parvenu* had wanted to acquire aristocratic table manners, but never progressed beyond a grotesquely comic use of his knife and fork. He was always ridiculous at table, I now thought, sitting in the wing chair, just as he was ridiculous in everything he did, and he became more ridiculous as time went on, because he constantly endeavored to do everything in an increasingly refined fashion, to make himself more refined, to apply whatever knowledge he acquired about so-called aristocratic manners in every sphere, and this in time made him seem not only increasingly comic and grotesque, but increasingly repellent, I thought as I sat in the wing chair. After he had hurled his insult in the direction of the kitchen, leaned back in his chair and stuck his tongue out at his wife, a pause intervened. Then he said suddenly, *I don't like Strindberg at all*, and looked around at the assembled company. At this point I jumped up and ostentatiously went to sit with John and the woman from the general store, thinking to myself, No, I don't want to have anything to do with this party. After joining John and the woman from the general store at their table, I heard Auersberger's wife say, *The Wild Duck is by Ibsen*. From then on I simply ignored the artists' table and ordered a glass of beer. I wanted to get more information out of John than he had already vouchsafed, not only about the transfer of the body, but about everything connected with Joana, and the woman from the general store was just as keen as I was to get him to tell us what his life with Joana had really been like. He told us that he had first met her in her apartment in the

Simmeringer Hauptstrasse, which she had converted into
what she called a *movement studio* in the mid-sixties. A
girl friend of his, who had taken lessons from Joana for
some time, took him along with her one day to Joana's
apartment in the Simmeringer Hauptstrasse so that he could
see what a good sport Joana was, or, as John put it, what
an artistic nature she had, as I recalled, sitting in the wing
chair. He had paid a second and then a third visit to Joana's
with his girl friend, and then he had started going alone,
without his girl friend, with whom he split up overnight
because of Joana. He had not taken lessons from her, he
said, but *found security* with her, and she had *found security*
with him. Basically he had no time for the *movement
studio,* as Joana called it; right from the start he had been
convinced that Joana used the movement studio simply
as a means to *keep herself above water from a personal point
of view,* as he put it, since there was nothing in it for her
from an *intellectual or financial point of view.* The only
people who went there were people with virtually no
means, young hopefuls in the acting profession and older
theatrical people who at the age of fifty or sixty had not
yet given up hope of a career, though naturally they no
longer had the slightest prospect of making one. After he
had slept with her several times he moved in as her lodger.
His real name was *Friedrich,* but Joana disliked the name,
and so from the beginning she had called him *not Friedrich,
but John,* and ever since then he had been *John* to everybody. He came from Schwarzach Sankt Veit, a rail junc-
tion I knew well, in the Salzburg province. His father
had been a railroad worker among other things. He had
gone to school at Sankt Johann, then to a technical college
in Salzburg. At the age of twenty-three he had gone to
Vienna, and to make ends meet he had worked for a film

company in Sievering, where he had got to know his previous girl friend, the one who introduced him to Joana, I recalled in the wing chair. At first he had pretended to Joana that he was interested in her movement lessons, though in fact he did not have the least interest in them, and to prove how great his interest was he had *hopped around a few times*, as he put it, with his girl friend, but then he had abandoned the pretense, giving Joana to understand at a fairly early stage that he was interested in her and not in her movement lessons. According to John she was not at all put out by this, I recalled in the wing chair. Joana earned no money, and by now more or less all her possessions had been sold. She got no support from her tapestry artist, not having heard from him since he had left her; all this time she had no idea whether or not he was still living in Mexico, or whether he was still with her friend who had gone with him to Mexico (according to John she used to speak of her friend's being *abducted*). He therefore took it upon himself to provide for her. She had continued to give lessons for another two years after he moved in with her, but finally, on his orders, she gave up the movement studio, which had brought nothing but unhappiness, vexation and dissension into their lives. Wanting to wean her off drink, he had paid for her to have *seven periods of treatment at the Kalksburg Clinic*, but all to no avail: no sooner had she returned from Kalksburg than she started drinking again, until in the end she became a *complete lush*, as he put it. But he did not desert her. He said he had *really loved her*, I recalled, sitting in the wing chair and looking into the music room; he said he had wanted to *care for* this *unhappy girl*, as he described her in the *Iron Hand. Joana was always an unhappy girl*, he said, as I now recalled, sitting in the wing chair; he repeated these words several times. I did not see it that way, for the Joana I had known was a happy person—at least she was happy in the fifties, I thought, and up to the mid-sixties, at any rate until the time when she was deserted by the tapestry artist. It was only then that unhappiness and misfortune closed in on her, I thought. John, however, had known her only as an unhappy girl whom he wanted to make happy, though he had not succeeded, I thought. He said several times, *I wanted to make Joana happy, but I failed.* The whole helplessness of his situation was summed up in this sentence, I thought, sitting in the wing chair. He told us that she often went to Kilb, not always with him; she often went back home, only to return to Vienna disillusioned. *At first* he'd tried to do it *by gentleness* and then *by firmness* (these were his own words), I recalled. But finally he realized that Joana could not be saved. On the evening before she killed herself she had said good-bye to him, as she always did when she went to Kilb. It was six in the morning when the woman from the general store had called him. She had told him *straight out, without beating about the bush,* that Joana had hanged herself, whereas with me she had behaved quite differently, not telling me straight out, but only gradually as I began to press her for details. She told John at once that Joana had killed herself, that she had hanged herself, but she did *not* tell me at once. I mulled this fact over for some time in the wing chair. She's more familiar with John than she is with me, I had thought as I sat with them in the *Iron Hand*, and immediately confided in him. To John she says directly what she thinks, but not to me: she speaks to me in a stilted and roundabout manner, as country people do when talking to people from the city, as so-called uneducated people do when talking to so-called educated people, as people who consider themselves inferior do when talking to their so-called betters. It had not surprised him, John suddenly said, turning to the woman from the general store, with whom he must have had fairly close contacts for some time, I reflected in the wing chair. He had put his winter overcoat on, slung his black bag over his shoulder, and come out to Kilb. What happened after that, he said, had been utterly depressing. If there was one person in Kilb today who truly mourned Joana and was genuinely shattered by her suicide, I thought, it was John, who is not at all as degenerate as I had thought all along. As I thought about this man I suddenly became aware that he had many good qualities and decided that, even though Joana had ultimately killed herself, he had been the saving of her, her *refuge*, somebody she could believe in, at any rate for seven or eight years, for without such a refuge she would probably have killed herself much earlier, I now reflected in the wing chair. Joana had wanted to achieve something special in Vienna, but according to John she couldn't break loose from Kilb, I thought, sitting in the wing chair. I cannot remember how she met Fritz, the tapestry artist. When I met her she had been married to him for some years, and I always believed that they were very happily married: at least this was the impression I always had when I visited them in the Sebastiansplatz. At times I actually thought of the apartment in the Sebastiansplatz, this big studio where I could do more or less as I pleased, as my home. Fritz and his wife Joana, née Elfriede, were a *focal point of Viennese artistic life*, where the so-called dramatic and the so-called plastic arts had entered upon a seemingly ideal marriage, and where all art—or what I then considered to be art—could come together.

At this studio in the Sebastiansplatz, in the mid-fifties, I met more or less all the significant Viennese artists and scholars who were well known at the time, though not necessarily famous—as well as all the pseudo-artists and pseudo-scholars—and it was among such people and through contact with them that I came to see myself as a writer in the making, even as a fellow artist. I had lodgings in the Nussdorferstrasse, in the Eighteenth District, where I spent my time sleeping, but it was in the Sebastiansplatz, in the Third District, that I had my *temple of art*, which I would enter at about five o'clock in the afternoon and not leave until about three in the morning. Fritz's looms, worked by two or three female assistants, were set up in enormous rooms, eighteen or twenty feet high; it was on these looms that he created his tapestries, which were already much sought after, at least by experts, all over Europe. It was quite by chance, Fritz said simply, that he had become a tapestry artist, having previously been a painter working in oils. He always gave the impression of being a quiet man who did not parade his intelligence and for whom a precise program of work was the be-all and end-all of existence: all the time I knew him he could never be deflected by anything or anybody from his eight-hour working day, I thought, sitting in the wing chair. He smoked a short English pipe, which he never removed from the corner of his mouth, not even when he was talking to you, which he was always reluctant to do when weaving, but always did without losing his cool, as they say. The English pipe remained in his mouth even when it had gone out and was completely cold. His brother was a highly esteemed Viennese architect, who built what are called major residential apartments on the outskirts of the city and whom his brother always referred to as *that brilliant*

urban vandal. Despite having grown up in a well-to-do
family with a town house and a more or less princely estate
in the wine-growing district of Baden, Fritz was a thoroughly
modest man, or so it appeared right up to the time when,
as already mentioned, he *bolted to Mexico.* It was not only
artists who gathered in the apartment in the Sebastiansplatz,
but so-called important people from every walk of life,
whom Joana would seek out and invite to visit them, on
the one hand to satisfy her already pathological need for
company, and on the other to ensure that her husband's
tapestries became increasingly well-known and increasingly
expensive. And so naturally newspaper critics and politicians were always being invited to the Sebastiansplatz;
this, it now strikes me, was precisely the kind of social
ambience I craved more than anything as a young man in
search of wider horizons. In the Sebastiansplatz I found, as
it were, an ideal cross-section of Viennese society, which
was necessary, indeed indispensable, to the up-and-coming
artist, and above all to the up-and-coming writer I fervently
believed myself to be, and I can say without hesitation that
the Sebastiansplatz suddenly afforded an important founda-
tion for my intellectual development, the course of which
was charted, as they say, once and for all in the early fifties.
Joana had all the attractiveness that beautiful women from
Vienna and its environs can possibly have, and her taste
served her purposes ideally, exercising a powerful magnetism
over the artistic, intellectual and political society of Vienna.
When she received her guests in the Sebastiansplatz, she
would wear long dresses of her own design (though not
of her own making), now in the Indian style, now in the
Egyptian, now in the Spanish, now in the Roman. At all
these receptions she displayed a gaiety of temperament
which was enhanced by a highly individual intelligence,

embodying as it were the artistic spirit of Vienna, and naturally captivated everyone who visited the Sebastiansplatz. Having attended two or three of her receptions, I suddenly became her favorite regular guest, so to speak. In those days no other address in Vienna exercised such a pull over me as the Sebastiansplatz, for I loved the studio, I loved Fritz the tapestry artist, and I loved Joana. Before I went to the Sebastiansplatz I had never seen a studio like this, such a large *theater of art*; I was fascinated by everything in the Sebastiansplatz, which for many years remained for me the very center of Vienna. Gradually I acquired what I may call a *conception of art*; I met all the artists, all the geniuses, as well as all those who were set upon becoming artists and geniuses. Observing Joana in the Sebastiansplatz, I was able to see how such a society *comports itself*, how it develops, how it is attracted, cultivated, nurtured and tamed, and how it can ultimately be abused and exploited. To put it in the simplest terms: in the Sebastiansplatz I studied society—and not only artistic society—and began to get a clear view of how it functioned. It was in the Sebastiansplatz that I first saw *what* artists were, *what they were like*, and *what made them what they were*. I also learned what they were not and never could be as long as they lived. In the Sebastiansplatz I was free to study them as I have never been able to since, with supreme intensity and hence with supreme receptivity, for at that time I was capable of the utmost intensity and receptivity. I may say that it was in the Sebastiansplatz that I first got to know human beings; I already knew them to some extent, better than many others in my position, but it was only in the Sebastiansplatz that I found out what human beings were really like, human beings of every kind, by making a conscious study of them. It was in the Sebastiansplatz that I began to evolve a method of watching and observing people which was to become my own personal art, an art which I was to practice for the rest of my life. It was in the Sebastiansplatz that I learned not only to admire human beings and human society, but also to despise them, I thought, to find them at once attractive and repellent. It was in the Sebastiansplatz that I first became clearly aware of the power and the impotence of artists, and of human beings in general; it was as though I was able at last to disperse the impenetrable fog that had hitherto blocked my view of so-called artistic society. Never before or since have I seen so many artists almost every day and every night as I did in the Sebastiansplatz, and all these artists—most of whom, it occurs to me, were probably what I would now call *non-artists*, and probably remained such—flitted in and out of the apartment in the Sebastiansplatz, while I *stayed* there nearly all the time, admiring Fritz as he sat dedicatedly working at his tapestries, and loving Joana as she dreamed of her future fame in the biggest of all Vienna's studios. Today, if I see some so-called celebrity mentioned in the newspapers, it is almost certain to be somebody I met in the Sebastiansplatz. Joana's fellow students who had studied and qualified with her at the Reinhardt Seminar had long since disappeared in the many theatrical cesspits that existed in Vienna in those days. Meanwhile Elfriede Slukal, in what she believed to be a moment of clairvoyance, decided to transform herself into Joana and become the wife of Fritz the tapestry artist. While her former colleagues had for years been forced into the nerve-racking business of pandering to a sick public with an insatiable appetite for entertainment, prostituting themselves to a brand of literature that can be described only as pathetic, it is possible that Joana had already given up her dreams of having her own career and was concentrating solely on furthering that of her tapestry artist. She staked her whole talent—not only an artistic talent, but her phenomenal *social talent*—on her devoted Fritz, and in this she was successful right from the start. For without Joana, Fritz would never have become the *international tapestry artist* he now is; he would certainly not have won the big prize in São Paulo for his *Associative Mountain Range*, and without Joana he would not be the famous professor who from time to time hits the headlines, as they say, in today's newspapers and magazines. Joana sacrificed herself for Fritz, it seems to me, and never recovered from her sacrifice; this was probably the cause of the lifelong despair she had to endure, without ever showing it, a despair which I think probably broke her, as they say, though not until eight or nine years after the collapse of her marriage, when she tried to find consolation with John, the commercial traveler. She made of Fritz what she had wanted to make of herself—a respected, celebrated and finally world-famous artistic personality. She forced him to the top because she could not force herself to the top; of the two of them it was *Fritz*, not she, who was actually cut out for world fame. From the moment she realized that she was not cut out for a career, let alone for an international career and international fame, she forced Fritz into a career, into an international career, into the straitjacket of an international career, as it now strikes me, but this brought her only temporary, not permanent, satisfaction. Without Joana, it seems to me, Fritz would have remained a charming pipe-smoking painter and carpet weaver, catering to middle-class demands, an affable fellow who was content with his work, his pipe and a glass of wine before he went to bed, either alone or in company. Joana more or less jolted him out of his mediocrity, first causing the artistic sap to rise and then bringing him into full bloom. But in the long run Joana could not be satisfied by Fritz's tapestries, which in due course hung in all the important museums and on the walls of executive suites in all the big industrial concerns, insurance companies and banks: the more well-known, the more famous his name and his art became, the more dejected she, the author of his success, was bound to be. When Fritz was at the zenith of his fame, Joana herself had naturally reached the nadir of dejection, but by now she could no longer break off her work, the building up and perfecting of her Fritz, at this high point in his career; Fritz was her one work of art, at which outwardly she continued to labor, progressively increasing its dimensions, though in her heart of hearts, as they say, she had long since come to hate it. It was, I think, this process of being perpetually forced to go on adding to the stature of her work of art and in doing so to push herself down to ever greater depths, that brought about her ruin. Joana was finally crushed, it seems to me, by the immense weight of the work that she had created and brought more or less to completion—by her beloved Fritz. What she had been unable to achieve in herself, namely the birth of a great artist, a so-called major artist, she achieved in the person of Fritz, and when the work had become reality and she saw what she had done, what she had on her conscience, it literally frightened her to death. If we cannot become what we want to become, we resort to another person—inevitably the person closest to us—and make of him what we have been unable to make of ourselves, Joana had probably thought, and so, I think, she fashioned Fritz into this colossal work of art which finally crushed and destroyed her. No one who knew Fritz would have thought it possible for him to become the world-famous artist he did become, or for his work to achieve the international acclaim it did achieve, for it was obvious to all that everything about him was *quite incompatible* with fame of such magnitude. Yet despite what everyone thought he did become a world-famous figure, thanks, I believe, to Joana. It was she, I believe, who transformed the honest unpretentious Fritz into the celebrated man of the world he is today, because she was able, through her absolute dedication, to invest in him everything she was forced to deny herself, a boundless and unquenchable thirst for fame. I have no hesitation in saying that Fritz is Joana's handiwork; I will go further and say that Fritz's art, the works he created, all the tapestries that now hang in famous museums throughout the world, are really Joana's, just as everything he is today derives from Joana, *is* Joana. But obviously nobody takes an idea like this seriously, even though of course such ideas, which are not taken seriously, are actually the only serious ideas and always will be. It is only in order to survive, it seems to me, that we have such serious ideas which are not taken seriously. What am I doing in this company, with which I have had no contact and have wanted no contact for twenty years, people who have gone their own way just as I have gone mine? I asked myself, sitting in the wing chair. What am I doing in the Gentzgasse? And I told myself that I had *momentarily yielded to sentimentality* in the Graben and that I should never have yielded to such disgraceful sentimentality. To think that I weakened for a moment in the Graben and made myself cheap by accepting an invitation from the Auersbergers, I said to myself, sitting in the wing chair, people whom I've despised and detested for so many years!

For no more than a moment we become disgustingly sentimental, I told myself in the wing chair, and commit the
crime of stupidity, going somewhere we ought never to go
and even visiting people we despise and detest, I thought,
sitting in the wing chair: I've actually come to the Gentzgasse, and this is without doubt not just an act of folly, but
conduct of the most contemptible kind. We become weak
and walk into the trap, into the social trap, I thought,
sitting in the wing chair, for to me this apartment in
the Gentzgasse is nothing but a social trap, and I've just
walked into it. For there can be no doubt that the Auersbergers feel nothing but hatred for me, and so do all the
other members of the party in the by now foul-smelling
music room, as they await the arrival of the actor from
the Burgtheater, who is enjoying *such a great success in
The Wild Duck*, as Auersberger's wife never tires of repeating, I thought, sitting in the wing chair. They've been
waiting for him longer than they'd ever have waited for
me, I thought. The actor's bound to make their evening,
I thought—this self-important theatrical blockhead! For the
sake of this disagreeable individual they've let themselves
be kept waiting over two hours for a supper which the
hostess insists on calling an *artistic dinner*, probably because that's what she's always called her dinners, though
I remember them only too clearly as *revolting dinners*, I
thought, sitting in the wing chair. Whether at Maria Zaal
or in the Gentzgasse, dinners at the Auersbergers' were
always more or less revolting; they always wanted to give
the grandest dinners and always convinced themselves that
they succeeded, but in reality their dinners were always
revolting and ridiculous, utterly ludicrous and unappetizing, I thought, sitting in the wing chair. They were always

meant to be the acme of refinement, but they always turned out to be the acme of tastelessness—they were intended to be the most splendid occasions, but they unfailingly turned out to be unmitigated disasters, I recalled in the wing chair. The food was supposed to be superb, yet what was dished up was always inadequate, I thought; whenever they gave a supper party they planned to serve the choicest food, but time and again what eventually arrived on the table fell so far short of what they had planned as to be positively embarrassing. Basically their suppers never worked out: the food was never particularly good, though it was often *quite* good, and the wine was never particularly good, or even *quite* good: it was uniformly bad—of poor quality and served either too warm or too cold, and it was always either too sweet or too dry, I recalled in the wing chair. And as hosts the Auersbergers always *came unstuck*, as they say, right at the beginning of any supper party or dinner party they gave: after the first two or three mouthfuls they would invariably rise to each other's dreadful provocations and drag their guests, willy-nilly, into the chaos of their personal lives. They never showed any consideration for their guests, whom they would start pelting quite shamelessly with their marital filth when they tired of merely pelting each other; in addition to the inadequate food they would dish up their own distasteful innards in front of the outraged guests, whom they finally drove away with their marital brawls, their mutual insults, and their torrents of mutual recrimination. I can remember scarcely a single supper with them, either at Maria Zaal or in the Gentzgasse, that did not culminate in some marital explosion; all their dinner parties—or rather supper parties —in the Gentzgasse would finally blow up, in the truest sense of the word, and at Maria Zaal they usually left behind a scene of conjugal carnage and a foul stench of unholiest matrimony, I thought, sitting in the wing chair and looking into the music room. The Auersbergers were perversely obsessed with their own social indigence, *she* because she came of a rather ridiculous family belonging to the Alpine gentry of Styria, *he* because his maternal grandfather had been a butcher's assistant at Feldbach and his father a petty local government official. This was no doubt why they always felt they had to hoist themselves up the social ladder, an effort that required all the energy they could muster and was always obvious to the eye of the trained observer, I thought, sitting in the wing chair. All her life she was constantly trying to escape from her origins, just as he was from his—she from the idyll of her gentle Styrian birth, he from the paternal destiny of petty local officialdom and the maternal low-pressure zone inhabited by butchers' assistants—all of which was bound to appear irresistibly comic to anyone around them who had eyes to see and ears to hear. She was forever trying, by every means at her command, to climb just one rung further up the ladder from her pathetic Styrian idyll into the higher echelons of rural barons and counts, though in all the years I have known the Auersbergers her endeavors were of no avail, for whenever she so much as got a grip on this higher rung of the nobility which she so fervently wished to reach, she was brutally and unceremoniously thrust down by those who occupied it, by the very people with whom she longed to be associated, and this, I know, caused her endless pain. She failed in all her attempts to reach this superior rung of the rural nobility and hold on to it—at least for a while, I thought, sitting in the wing chair, for she knew that she could not hold on forever. Her outfits did her no good, I thought, sitting in the wing chair, nor did her husband's do him any good. His attempts at upward mobility into the aristocracy came to grief even more pitifully and calamitously than hers. It was, as I know, his life's ambition to be an aristocrat, nothing less: the sad truth is that he would rather have been a witless aristocrat than a respectable composer. As long as I have known him he has always dressed like a Styrian count, and of course he would never be seen without the ostentatious signet ring on his left hand. He has always cut a ludicrous figure; though not lacking in wit, as people always remarked, he was a hopeless figure of fun. Auersberger isn't stupid—anything but, I thought, sitting in the wing chair—but in this one respect, his desire to be an aristocrat, a count at the very least, he was always the most idiotic of social climbers, I thought as I sat in the wing chair. At Kilb he made himself look vulgar and ridiculous by screaming *This food's abominable*, in the same way, it now occurred to me, as he's made himself look vulgar and ridiculous hundreds and thousands of times in my presence. Whenever he straightened his neck and pursed his little lips to pass sentence of death on food or drink or some other trifling matter, what came out was not witty, but pathetic—merely foolish and distasteful. And the most distasteful thing of all about him is that, although officially he is called Auersberger—which is naturally what I have always called him—he once decided, in an access of *folie de grandeur*, to call himself *Auersberg*: on first meeting his future wife, the daughter of the country gentry, in the Gentzgasse (where, as I happen to know, she started off as his landlady), he decided to chop off his tail—in other words the last syllable of his surname—and proceeded to call himself *Auersberg*, in order to give the impression that he belonged to the ancient princely family of that name. Were *revolting* not the proper term to describe this perverse castration of his own name, one would have to ignore all the rules of the game and call it simply pathetic, I thought, sitting in the wing chair. Auersberger's conduct at Kilb was no different from what I was accustomed to when we knew each other in the fifties. He hasn't changed in the least, I thought, sitting in the wing chair. In the *Iron Hand*, after two or three glasses of wine, he began to play the clown for the benefit of all the people at his table, I thought, putting on his infantile circus act as he once more became conscious of his central role, and *upstaging everyone else*, as they say. And when he said, *This food's abominable*, I went to sit with John and the woman from the general store, because I found both the Auersbergers, in their different ways, quite insufferable. Hardly had I set eyes on them in their tasteless clothes— her in her blue print Styrian dirndl and him in his Styrian linen jacket—than I felt sick, realizing at once that neither had changed since we had last known one another—that the last twenty years, which had wrought such enormous changes in the world, had passed these people by without leaving so much as a trace. How pathetic and repellent the Auersbergers were, sitting at their table in the *Iron Hand*, I thought as I sat in the wing chair, yet they were still surrounded by all their friends from the old days, as though they were the center of some magic circle. No matter how ridiculous and how worthless this couple may be, I thought, sitting in the wing chair, they still have the same hangers-on as they had in the fifties, twenty or thirty years ago. It was as though nothing had changed in the last twenty years: the Auersbergers were once more surrounded by the same artistic coterie that had surrounded them thirty years ago. What can the reason be? I wondered, sitting in the wing chair. But I could find no answer. I was suddenly intrigued by the question of how this couple, neither of whom earned any money, could still continue to exist, and it struck me how inexhaustible their wealth must originally have been, for after thirty-five years of marriage it still not only protected them and kept them alive, but enabled them to lead a life of self-indulgence. Auersberger himself had nothing but his original genius, I thought, sitting in the wing chair, a quite remarkable musical gift, as well as an immense verbal talent, and a quite extraordinary intelligence bordering on insanity, yet he hadn't a penny to his name, except for the pittance he had earned for years as a teacher at the Vienna Conservatory before his marriage. His wife, by contrast, whose maiden name was *von Reyer*, came from a family I had always assumed to be fairly affluent, but now know to have been really rich. One of the sources of her wealth was a number of plots of land around Maria Zaal which her father had bought for a song between the wars, among them the so-called *manor house*, a five-hundred-year-old building that had once belonged to the provincial government of Salzburg. It was here that the couple spent the whole of the summer when the Gentzgasse became too stifling and oppressive; like all affluent Viennese, they would escape to the country for the summer, though unlike most they did not wait until late July, but left the capital at the end of May. Their property is all situated around Maria Zaal, which used to be one of the most beautiful villages in Styria, famous especially for its large church, formerly a place of pilgrimage, an architectural jewel, part Romanesque, part Gothic, which the local people respectfully call the *minster*. The Auersbergers have been living off their property for almost thirty-five years by gradually selling it off, I thought, sitting in the wing chair. An uncle of hers, a well-known Styrian lawyer, has been parceling it off and disposing of it for them by degrees. It's heartbreaking to see what's become of Maria Zaal through the sale of the Auersbergers' property, I thought, sitting in the wing chair. Where twenty years ago there were the most beautiful fields and meadows there are now dozens of detached houses, each as ugly as the next and mostly prefabricated, which purchasers can order direct from various warehouses in the vicinity, horrid little concrete cubes with roofs made of cheap corrugated asbestos concrete and nailed to the main structure by incompetent local contractors. Where there was once a copse or a thicket, where a garden once blossomed in spring and its glorious colors faded in the fall, there is now a rank growth of the concrete tumors beloved of our modern age, which no longer has any thought for landscape or nature, but is consumed by politically motivated greed and by the base proletarian mania for concrete, I thought, sitting in the wing chair. Every year one or more of the Auersbergers' properties are sold off to people who are gradually ruining Maria Zaal. In fact it is ruined already, as I saw for myself when I passed through two or three years ago—incognito as it were—on my way back from Italy to Vienna. I could hardly believe my eyes, I recalled in the wing chair, when I saw the extent to which Maria Zaal had been destroyed simply through the sale of the Auersbergers' land. Each time a plot of land is sold by the Auersbergers—who do not earn any money, doubtless because they think they have no need to—a bit of the natural landscape around Maria Zaal is destroyed. Maria Zaal is actually destroyed already, for the truth is that, having been one of the most beautiful villages in Styria twenty years ago, it is now one of the ugliest, thanks to the gross irresponsibility of the Auersbergers, I thought, sitting in the wing chair. They have this Styrian jewel on their consciences, I thought, and it suddenly occurred to me that the blame for the spoliation of the countryside around Maria Zaal lay not with the little people of the region, whom our revolting age has infected with building hysteria, but with the Auersbergers—not with the people who are usually blamed, whose repulsive houses have wreaked havoc throughout almost the whole area around this once unique village, who have simply *shat out* their houses into the landscape—not just here, but throughout Austria—because they have never been told how to build properly: the blame lay with the Auersbergers lurking in the background, who every year persuade their obliging uncle to sell off one or two of the remaining plots so that they can go on leading their more or less futile social life without having to lift a finger, I thought as I sat in the wing chair. *Perfidious society masturbators*—what an apt description! I thought, sitting in the wing chair and recalling how Fritz the tapestry artist had once used it to their faces. Auersberger wanted to be a composer, yet this successor of Webern has become nothing but a degenerate *society ape* who's grown stupid on the proceeds of his wife's fortune. Seldom have I been so enraged by the Auersbergers as I was that evening. People like Joana kill themselves, I thought, sitting in the wing chair, while parasites and society apes like the Auersbergers live on and on and on, getting older and older and older, boring themselves out of their minds all their lives and remaining utterly futile. People like Joana end up with self-tied nooses around their necks and are stuffed into plastic bags and dumped in the ground as cheaply as possible, while people like the Auersbergers don't know how many dinner parties to give for how many Burgtheater actors in order to survive their sickening boredom and their mindless world-weariness, I thought, sitting in the wing chair. People like Joana have to be content for years with the bare necessities of life and finally kill themselves, while people like the Auersbergers have everything in abundance and reach a ripe old age to no purpose, I thought. A person like Joana is finally abandoned by all these people, because they can no longer be bothered with her, yet they continue to flock around people like the Auersbergers just as they did twenty years ago. These dinners given by the Auersbergers are just part of a perverse routine, I told myself, sitting in the wing chair. This couple has a house in the country and throws it open to all this artistic riffraff from the capital who are eager for a breath of country air, not out of philanthropy—naturally not— but out of sickening boredom and crass self-interest. They use all these people, who continue to turn up under the guise of old friendship, for their own purposes, offending, abusing and demoralizing them, just as for years they offended, abused and demoralized me, and all this Viennese artistic riffraff, as I chose to call the people who were standing or sitting around in the music room, actually come to the Gentzgasse to show their *gratitude*. Like me, all these people standing or sitting around in the music room were guests of the Auersbergers at Maria Zaal for years, letting themselves be used by their hosts, helping them cope with their rural boredom, and joining in their rural extravagances for days, weeks, months and years, without realizing that they were being violated, exploited and abused by the Auersbergers. They were invited in order to be abused, they weren't invited out of friendship or affection or what-

ever other absurd motive the Auersbergers alleged, I thought,
sitting in the wing chair. The Auersbergers invited me to
Maria Zaal to paper over the cracks of their ramshackle
marriage, not, as they pretended, to give me a holiday.
They thought I would be able to disentangle the knots in
their marriage—though of course they didn't say anything about this. They made out that they wanted to
spoil me for a few weeks or months, even for *a whole
year* or for *two years*, but this was by no means all they
wanted. The first time they invited me to Maria Zaal I
may have seemed run down, neglected and half starved,
but they did not invite me there to nurse me back to
health: they quite unscrupulously lured me into their trap
at Maria Zaal to make their matrimonial hell endurable—
not because I was an undernourished youth in need of
care and affection, but because they saw me as a means to
an end, a Salzburg clown they had discovered who would
rescue *them* from the hell of their marriage. And I was too
naive to recognize the trap they set for me, and so I
groped my way into it and at once started playing the
Salzburg fool for them in their frightful Styrian retreat—
and I went on playing the fool more and more, I now
reflected as I sat in the wing chair. I remember how, when
I left the Mozarteum, I screwed up my diploma into a
sticky ball with both hands and stuffed it in my trouser
pocket, and then at Fritz's birthday party in the Sebastiansplatz they invited me to Maria Zaal, I recalled in the wing
chair, and I accepted their invitation because I did not
know I was being invited to their matrimonial hell. They
pounced unscrupulously on the naive youth from Salzburg
and invited him to their residence at Maria Zaal. And I
accepted their invitation, only later realizing that it had
been madness to do so. People like the Auersbergers tell us

that they have money and a beautiful big estate, an enormous estate with a beautiful big house on it, an enormous house, and as we ourselves have none of these things, we walk into their trap, I thought. We let ourselves be impressed by their wealth and walk into their trap. Seeing only the facade and taking all they say at its face value, we walk into their trap, I thought, sitting in the wing chair. They tell us about a big, old house with fine vaulting, about long walks in grounds that all belong to them, about delicious meals in their garden and daily car trips from one castle to another, and, being impressed, we walk into their trap. They describe a rustic life of absolute luxury, and, being impressed, we walk into their luxurious rustic trap, I thought, sitting in the wing chair. Again and again they talk about the things they own, *about their endless wealth*, though not in so many words, and we let ourselves be impressed and walk into their trap. They talk about their well-furnished kitchens and their well-stocked cellars and the thousands of volumes in their libraries, and, letting ourselves be impressed, we walk into their trap. They tell us about their stock ponds and their water mills and their sawmills, but not about their beds, and we are impressed by them and fall into their trap—and into their beds, I thought. And if we have more or less come to the end of the road, as I had in the early fifties, and don't know where to go next, we allow ourselves to be *profoundly impressed by them* and are only too glad to walk into their trap. I had been at a loss to know what to do when I left the Mozarteum, and so I went to Vienna, but Vienna offered me no escape—only cold, brutal hopelessness—and so naturally I walked into the Auersbergers' trap, and it proved almost fatal, I thought, sitting in the wing chair. Their instinct was unerring, I thought, in the early fifties: I was the best possible bet for the Auersbergers, whom I first met at that time, though suddenly I don't know how or where I met them. I know I met Joana in the Sebastiansplatz through Jeannie Billroth, I now recalled, but I no longer know where I met the Auersbergers. I suddenly asked myself, Where *did* I meet them? But I no longer knew—I had forgotten. I kept trying to remember, but it was no good. I've often had such momentary spells of debility recently, spells of mental debility, I thought, sitting in the wing chair, and it was hardly surprising in view of all my illnesses, all my nervous illnesses—and after what I had been through that day, I thought. And I told myself that this year alone, which was not a very long time, I had attended the funerals of *five* of my friends. They're all dying off one after the other, I thought, most of them by taking their own lives. They rush out of a coffeehouse in a state of sudden agitation, and are run over in the street, or else they hang themselves, or suffer a fatal stroke. When we're over fifty we're constantly going to funerals, I thought. I'll soon have more friends in the cemetery than in the rest of the city, I thought. People who were born in the country go back to the country to kill themselves, I thought. They choose to commit suicide in their parents' home, I thought. All of them, without exception, are basically sick. If they don't kill themselves they die of some illness that they've brought on through their own negligence. I repeated the word *negligence* to myself several times; I kept on repeating the word—it was as if the word gave me pleasure as I sat in the wing chair—until the people in the music room noticed, and when I saw them all looking in my direction I stopped repeating it. They were all friends of mine thirty years ago, I thought, and I could no longer understand why. For a time we go in the same direction as other people, then one day we wake up and turn our backs on them. I turned my back on these people—they didn't turn their backs on me, I thought. We attach ourselves to certain people, then suddenly we hate them and let go. We run after them for years, begging for their affection, I thought, and when once we have their affection we no longer want it. We flee from them and they catch up with us and seize hold of us, and we submit to them and all their dictates, I thought, surrendering to them until we either die or break loose. We flee from them and they catch up with us and crush us to death. We run after them and implore them to accept us, and they accept us and do us to death. Or else we avoid them from the beginning and succeed in avoiding them all our lives, I thought. Or we walk into their trap and suffocate. Or we escape from them and start running them down, slandering them and spreading lies about them, I thought, in order to save ourselves, slandering them wherever we can in order to save ourselves, running away from them for dear life and accusing them everywhere of having *us* on their consciences. Or they escape from us and slander and accuse us, spreading every possible lie about us in order to save themselves, I thought. We think our lives are finished, and then we chance to meet them and they rescue us, but we are not grateful to them for rescuing us: on the contrary we curse them and hate them for rescuing us, and we pursue them all our lives with the hatred we feel toward them for having rescued us. Or else we try to curry favor with them and they push us away, and so we avenge ourselves by slandering them, running them down wherever we can and pursuing them to their graves with our hatred. Or they help us back on our feet at the crucial moment and we hate them for it, just as they hate us when we help them back on their feet, I thought as I sat in the wing chair. We do them a favor and then think we are entitled to their eternal gratitude, I thought, sitting in the wing chair. For years we are on terms of friendship with them, then suddenly we no longer are, and we don't know why. We love them so fervently that we become positively lovesick, and they reject us and hate us for our love, I thought. We're nothing, and they make something of us, and we hate them for it. We come from nowhere, as people say, and they perhaps make a genius out of us, and we never forgive them for it, just as if they'd made a dangerous criminal out of us, I thought as I sat in the wing chair. We take everything they have to give us, I thought, sitting in the wing chair, and we punish them with a life sentence of contempt and hatred. We owe everything to them and never forgive them for the fact that we owe everything to them, I thought. We think we have rights when we have no rights of any kind, I thought. No one has any rights, I thought. There's nothing but injustice in the world, I thought. Human beings are unjust, and injustice prevails everywhere —that's the truth, I thought. Injustice is all we have to hand, I thought. These people have never done anything but pretend to be something, while in reality they've never been anything: they pretend to be educated, but they're not; they pretend to be artistic (as they call it), but they're not; and they pretend to be humane, but they're not, I thought. And their supposed kindness was only pretense, for they were never kind. And above all they pretended to be natural, and they were never natural: everything about them was artificial, and when they claimed—in other words, pretended—to be philosophical, they were nothing but eccentric, and it struck me again how repellent they had seemed to me in the Graben when they told me they now had bought *everything by Wittgenstein*, just as twenty-five years earlier they had said they had bought *everything by Ferdinand Ebner*, with just the same tasteless pretense to a knowledge of philosophy—or at least to an interest in philosophy—because they thought they had to for my benefit, since they believed then—and probably still do—that I have a philosophical bent, that I am a philosophizer —which I am not, for to this day I really have no idea what the words *philosopher* and *philosophize* mean. At various times they pretended to know about French or Spanish or German literature. And it is of course true that I got to know the works of many Spanish and French writers, as well as most German writers, while I was staying with them, especially at Maria Zaal, where they have an enormous library, much bigger than the one in the Gentzgasse, though this too is fairly substantial—what one might call a representative library, even a scholar's library, founded by the great-grandfather of Auersberger's wife, also for show. The Auersbergers, who inherited this library, have probably taken out no more than twenty or thirty volumes in the past thirty years, whereas I positively fell upon these collections in the Gentzgasse and Maria Zaal with all the passion of the ignoramus, as I have to admit. And perhaps what tied me to the Gentzgasse and Maria Zaal was not so much the Auersbergers themselves as the extensive libraries which their forebears had founded merely for show, a show of scholarship, culture and comprehensive knowledge—the kind of wide-ranging knowledge that is deemed to go with metropolitan life—things that have always been in fashion. There has never, I think, been a time when it was not fashionable to pretend to comprehensive knowledge, and even if it has become somewhat less fashionable in the last two decades, it is now all the rage again. They've always gone in for show, I thought, because they lack any capacity for reality. Everything about them has always been show: their social relations amount to nothing but show, and the same is true of their relations with each other, their marital relations: they've always put on a show of marriage because they've never been capable of sustaining a real one, I thought, sitting in the wing chair. And it's not only the Auersbergers who've always lived a life of pretense: all these people in the music room have only ever made a pretense of living— they've never really lived, they've never for one moment led a real life, a life that had any link with reality. They've never had the courage or the strength or the love of truth that is required for real living. They've always lived *in accordance with fashion*, I thought, cloaking themselves in fashion and becoming slaves to fashion for the sake of show, I thought. When it was fashionable in Vienna to read Ferdinand Ebner they read Ferdinand Ebner, just as today, when it's fashionable to read Wittgenstein, they read Wittgenstein, but of course they didn't really read Ferdinand Ebner then, and they don't really read Wittgenstein today. Thirty years ago they went out and bought Ebner's works, just as today they go out and buy Wittgenstein's; they talk about them but don't read them, and they continue to talk about them, without reading them, until suddenly what they've been talking about continually—sometimes for years—goes out of fashion, and all at once they stop talking about it. Wittgenstein is now talked about in Vienna as much as Ferdinand Ebner once was, yet it seems to me that Wittgenstein was more a philosopher than a teacher and Ferdinand Ebner more a teacher than a philosopher, and that Wittgenstein will survive and go down in history as a philosopher, unlike Ferdinand Ebner, who has already gone down in history simply as a teacher. The Auersbergers always made a show of being grand, just as they made a show of being artistic, and of course above all they always made a show of being humane, indeed hyper-humane, I thought, though beneath all this show they were never *capable* of being anything but pathetic: they could never be what they really *wanted* to be—first-class citizens, aristocrats—and members of the highest ranks of the aristocracy at that. What was so grotesque about them was that they remained constantly wedded to this comic but distasteful view of the world and let themselves be worn down by it day and night. They also made a show of patronizing the arts, however, and whenever they invited anyone, no matter whom, from outside the ranks of the aristocracy, they felt this to be an act of patronage, I thought. In the end I dubbed them *rural patrons of the arts*—a kind of ironic carnival title, but they took this bitter jest of mine at face value. Instead of traveling *extensively*, instead of broadening their minds by *extensive* travel, as they could so easily have afforded to do with all their money, they wasted all their time—whole decades of their lives—aping the upper crust and endeavoring to be aristocrats. These sedulous apes exhausted themselves in this aristocratic mania of theirs, of which they could not be cured and had no wish to be cured, I thought. They made a show of being artistic, yet remained essentially petit bourgeois, too feeble to behave like members of the true bourgeoisie, let alone its upper reaches, which they feebly affected to despise, I thought. And so they exploited to the utmost anyone who walked into their trap, I thought. But the people they exploited had no one to blame but themselves, I thought, for they were fully aware that they were being exploited and derived the greatest benefit from it. The victims of the Auersbergers' exploitation did indeed benefit from it, just as I did for years. It would be true to say that this exploitation eventually had the same effect as a health cure: the Auersbergers' exploitation cure finally brought me back to health, I thought. Having been thoroughly sick in both mind and body when I first met them thirty years ago, I regained my health, though not my happiness, through submitting to the Auersbergers' exploitation cure, I thought as I sat in the wing chair. They rescued me thirty years ago, I thought, but I also rescued them—that's the truth. Now they're pretending that they're giving their *artistic dinner* for the artists they've invited, whereas in reality they're giving it for their own miserable selves. Ostensibly they're giving it for the actor, who, being an actor from the Burg-theater, allows himself to be fêted everywhere, just as all Burgtheater actors allow themselves to be fêted every-where and all the time in every corner of the city— ostensibly they're giving this party for the highly success-ful and highly acclaimed *star of The Wild Duck*, for Ekdal, but really they're giving it simply for themselves—osten-sibly the dinner is being given for the guests, but as always it's being given for the hosts, I thought, sitting in the wing chair. They've bought masses of food, all to be cooked and dished up for their artistic guests, yet it's actually been bought and cooked for themselves, and then they'll call this *artistic dinner* of theirs a contribution to the patronage of the arts. For weeks on end they'll tell everybody in

Vienna that they gave a dinner for the actor who played Ekdal in *The Wild Duck*, but what they won't tell them is that he accepted their invitation only after they'd begged him for weeks, and that in order to get hold of him they'd almost torn themselves apart, as they say in Vienna. They'll tell people that they gave a dinner, an *artistic dinner*, for the Burgtheater actor, as well as for a host of other artists who are not quite as distinguished as the actor, but nonetheless great artists, people who are also artists, artistic also-rans, one might say. They say they're giving a dinner for this actor, yet in all probability he agreed to come only under duress, for there's an element of blackmail in all their invitations, I thought, sitting in the wing chair. They owe their entire social life to blackmail, I thought: whatever social show they put on, it's always contrived by blackmail. Even if people go to their dinner parties more or less of their own free will, I thought, the Auersbergers still put them under a certain degree of duress. They'd much rather be entertaining aristocrats at their dinner table in the Gentzgasse, or at least people they take to be aristocrats, instead of the people who are here this evening, I thought, sitting in the wing chair. They'd rather be entertaining some seedy prince or degenerate count and his hangers-on than *these artistic folk*, of whom they've always had a horror; for they've never really been keen on anything artistic: they've only ever put on a show of being artistic, I thought, just as they're putting on this supper party as an *artistic dinner*, as a kind of show in other words. They're probably thinking that even if they don't have a prince or a count at their dinner table, they *do at least have an actor from the Burgtheater*, I thought, sitting in the wing chair, at the very moment when the actor arrived. People always refer to this man as a *Burgtheater actor*, because he has been playing at the Burgtheater for the last thirty or forty years. At dinner I was placed opposite Jeannie Billroth, the person I had found so revolting that afternoon at Kilb. They had all taken their places in the dining room before I was asked to the table—I was summoned so late, in fact, that I could only assume that they had forgotten about me, as they probably had. I had actually dozed off for a few moments in the wing chair, out of exhaustion, and woke up only when I was called to the dining room, that exquisite Empire monstrosity of theirs. Auersberger's wife came into the anteroom to summon me to dinner. She must have spent some time trying to rouse me, for when I first heard her call my name I was at once aware that she must have called it several times already. She was about to shake my shoulder to wake me, but I forestalled her and pushed her hand away, perhaps a little roughly. In the semidarkness of the anteroom I could not see the expression on her face, but I think I must have offended her by my somewhat abrupt reaction. However, I immediately got up and followed her into the dining room, where, as I have said, they had all taken their places, with the Burgtheater actor in the place of honor. I now realized that I had slept through his entrance. I had not heard him come in, and since he would have had to walk right in front of me to reach the dining room and I had not heard him, I realized that I must have been asleep, presumably for several minutes, possibly even for half an hour or longer. When I took my place at the table I was still somewhat dazed. I watched the cook bring in the soup—an absurd procedure at a quarter to one in the morning, I thought. They all ate hurriedly, listening to what the actor had to say as he spooned up his soup. It had not been *a good night*, he said: *Not my best night*, as he put it. Several times the audience at the Burgtheater had shouted *Speak up, speak up,* no doubt because he was speaking his lines too softly. He did not know why—it sometimes happened that an actor became so completely absorbed in his art while performing on stage that he entirely forgot about the audience, whereas the audience wanted not only to see him, but to hear him and understand what he said. He eats his soup as clumsily as he acts, I thought, though my eyes were not on the actor, but on Jeannie Billroth. She, on the other hand, was watching him and apparently taking in everything he said as he hurriedly spooned up his soup, as though what he had to say were something quite extraordinary, something unique. I found myself sitting opposite the Virginia Woolf of Vienna, this creator of tasteless poetry and prose who has never done anything throughout her life, it seems to me, but wallow in her petit bourgeois kitsch. And someone like this dares to say that she has surpassed Virginia Woolf, whom I consider the greatest of all women writers and have admired for as long as I have been competent to form a literary judgment—somebody like this has the temerity to assert that in her own novels she has surpassed *The Waves, Orlando* and *To the Lighthouse.* Jeannie showed herself once more in her true petit bourgeois colors when we were at Kilb, I now reflected, sitting opposite her and cursing this grotesque and distasteful *artistic dinner,* which was now, thanks to the Burgtheater actor, a late-night *artistic supper.* To serve potato soup at a quarter to one in the morning and announce that a boiled pike is to follow is a perversion of which only the Auersbergers are capable, I said to myself, sitting opposite Jeannie, who had always had her own special way of eating soup, with the little finger of her right hand sticking up about half an inch above the others.

Imagine serving a pike at a quarter to one in the morning in honor of an actor from the Burgtheater! The actor had already spooned up half his potato soup with great rapidity, *as though he were famished*, with such rapidity that some of it was now lodged in his beard. Ekdal, he said, spooning up his soup, has been my *dream role* for decades. And then he went on, interrupting himself after every other word to spoon up more soup, *Ekdal*—pause for a spoonful—*has always*—another spoonful—*been my*—another spoonful—*favorite part*, adding, after two more spoonfuls, *for decades*. And the phrase *dream role* he actually pronounced as though it denoted some culinary delicacy. *Ekdal is my favorite role*, he said several times, and I immediately wondered whether he would have said that Ekdal was his favorite role had he had no success in it. When an actor is successful in a certain role he says it's his favorite: when he isn't, he doesn't, I thought. The actor went on spooning up his soup and repeating that Ekdal was his favorite role. For a long time none of the other guests said anything, but merely ate their soup and stared at the actor, as though he were the only one entitled to speak. When he ate fast, they ate fast; when he slowed down, they slowed down; and by the time he had finished the last spoonful, so had they. Long after they had finished their soup I still had half a plateful left. I did not like the taste, and so I did not eat it. He had always wanted to play in *The Wild Duck*, and now at last he had the chance, the actor said with some pathos. If the other members of the cast had been better, if he had had ideal fellow actors in other words, he said— for they were not the best, they were not ideal; apart from himself the casting had been *a makeshift affair*—the production of *The Wild Duck* would have been *an enormous success as a whole* and not just where he was concerned.

As it was, everybody had concentrated on *his* performance; the newspapers had written exclusively about *him*. It was not *The Wild Duck*, not the production as such, that had been the great theatrical event, but his performance as Ekdal. *Where would The Wild Duck be, where would Ibsen be*, were it not for him?—that was more or less what all the papers had asked if one read between the lines. He himself had a high regard for Ibsen, just as he had for Strindberg, indeed for all the so-called Nordic dramatists, but where would these dramatists be without actors like himself? He asked this in all modesty, he said, but at the same time quite openly. But of course in his opinion there was more to these dramatists than the papers made out, he said: quite irrespective of whether the acting was superb or not, Ibsen was a great writer, and so was Strindberg—they were both *towering geniuses, towering figures in literary history, but where would they be without superb actors?* He must have had at least two or three glasses of champagne on arrival, I thought when I heard him say, Drama comes to life only *when a good actor brings it to life*. Whereupon he placed his hands on the table, raised his histrionic head, and said to Auersberger, *I greatly enjoyed your new composition, my dear friend*. At this Auersberger lowered his head; the successor of Webern lowered his head at the same moment as the actor raised his and paid his compliment. The whole company now fell silent, thinking that the pike was about to be brought in, but they were wrong: all that happened was that the cook entered the room empty-handed to ask whether the pike could now be served. The hosts indicated that it could. We actors are accustomed to dining late, the guest of honor remarked. We don't usually dine until after midnight. It's a typical feature of our profession that we don't dine until after midnight. It's an unhealthy life, the life of the theater, he added, breaking a pretzel stick in two. But an actor gets used to eating after midnight, he said. The role of Ekdal, more than any other, was his dream role, he said. You have to have great writing if you're to give a consummate performance. He had studied the role for a whole six months, the actor went on, and in order to carry out *this study of Ekdal* he had *withdrawn to a remote alpine chalet in the Tyrol*, for it was only *in such genuine solitude* that he was able to *understand the role properly*. Actors tended to approach a part either too early or too late, he said, and a part like Ekdal had to be *approached at just the right moment. Great drama and great dramatic roles must always be approached at just the right moment.* Ekdal was always my dream role, he said, but I'd never understood it properly. It was only when I was in the mountain chalet, concentrating solely on Ekdal, that I discovered the true nature of the character—and of *The Wild Duck* as a whole. *The true nature of The Wild Duck!* he exclaimed. It was in the mountain chalet, he said, that he had suddenly understood Ekdal. It was there, in the mountain chalet, that I saw the light, he said. Whereupon he leaned back and remarked that he had always been partial to pike—*preferably from Lake Balaton, the genuine Balaton pike.* Auersberger's wife now interrupted his disquisition on Ekdal to say that naturally she would never serve any pike other than a Balaton pike—what other pike was there? One has to approach Ekdal with great sensitivity, the actor said. We rush around in the city for months on end, racking our brains, yet failing to understand Ekdal or relate to the character in any way, despite the fact that in the whole of world literature we've always felt him to be the figure who most appeals to us, and we finally give up in despair, he said. And then we go up the mountain and live in the alpine chalet, and we see the light. *I had the same experience with Prospero*, the actor went on. *If I ever play Lear*, he said, *I shall go back to the chalet, and I won't spend months beforehand waiting around for enlightenment in this dreadful city*. It was the Tyrolean atmosphere, the actor said, that had revealed the secret of Ekdal to him—living in a chalet, five and a half thousand feet above sea level, far from civilization. *No electric light, no gas, no consumer society!* he exclaimed as a warm plate was placed before him and he was invited to help himself to the pike. *We must all scale the mountain heights if we are to get a proper view of the world*, he said, helping himself to a second portion of pike. Incidentally, he said, he had never played Ibsen before—Strindberg yes, Edgar in *The Dance of Death*, but never Ibsen. He had not even played Peer Gynt when he was a young man, though that would have been an obvious part for him to play. We come up against so many producers, he said, and they never give us the parts we really want to play. Or the dramatists who are *close to our hearts*. We want to act in a Spanish play and we're landed with a French one, he said. We want to play Goethe and we're condemned to play Schiller. We want to appear in comedy, and we're pushed into tragedy. Even being famous doesn't ensure that you always get the parts you want to play, the actor went on. And how often is one promised a part, one of one's favorite parts, he said, only to learn later that it's been given to somebody else! Theaters don't plan properly; nothing in the theater ever turns out according to plan. What's finally presented to the public is always a compromise, a sloppy compromise. By his age, he said, actors like himself had long since learned to live with all this. *Even at the Burgtheater, Europe's premier theater,*

as he put it, *all we get is compromises. But what compromises!* he said, implying that *the compromises reached
at the Burgtheater still constituted great theater.* Any accidents that happened there were after all Burgtheater
accidents, he said, implying that when all was said and done
the Burgtheater was a great theater, despite repeated disasters. What he said was quite ludicrous. I was so tired that
I could hardly keep my eyes open, but the actor was
obviously not at all tired. The rest of us were exhausted
after attending Joana's funeral and then spending more
than two hours waiting for the actor to make his appearance.
To think that you have to devote a whole six months to a
part like Ekdal, he said, and that during these six months
you have to give up everything else! *A role like Ekdal
completely takes you over,* robbing you of all creature
comforts while you're studying it (this was the word he
used), for after all it's not much fun locking oneself away
for weeks in a chalet in the Tyrol for the sake of Ekdal,
living on virtually nothing but bread and water and pea
soup, sleeping in an uncomfortable bed and hardly ever
washing—the audience has no idea about all this and gives
one no credit for it. *And even if they applaud and the role
is a great success, as Ekdal was this time,* he said, *the price
one pays for such devotion—I might even say for such
sacrifice—is too high.* But then an actor's life was *a life of
sacrifice,* he said, trying to insert a note of irony into the
remark but not succeeding, since it was clear to all that
it was meant seriously. Such a role, he said, required an
actor to give his all. *First getting inside the work,* he said,
*but how? Then arriving at a proper understanding of the
writer, then of the part, and then the long period of rehearsals,* which in this case had taken up the whole of the
fall and the winter. We begin rehearsing at the end of

August, and when rehearsals are completed we're not aware
that spring has come around again. With Shakespeare it's
quite different, he said, without telling us what it was that
made Shakespeare different from Ibsen. Or Strindberg. During the rehearsal period, unless he happened to be acting
in another play and had to appear on stage, he went to
bed at ten and got up at six. He *memorized* his lines, incidentally, in front of the *open window*, pacing up and
down in his bedroom. Being unmarried has always been an
advantage, he said suddenly. I walk to and fro in my bedroom more or less from seven o'clock to eleven and mem-
orize the text. I arrive at the first rehearsal having learned
the whole text, he said. Producers are always amazed at
this. Most actors turn up for rehearsals without knowing
their lines, he said. I always have all my lines in my head
when rehearsals begin. It's sickening when one's colleagues
don't know their lines. Sickening, he repeated as he helped
himself to more of the pike, which was served with a sauce
containing far too many capers. If I hadn't built myself a
house in Grinzing in 1954, he said, I might have gone on
the German stage—who knows? I had *numerous* offers. I
could have gone to Berlin, to Cologne, to Zurich. But what
are all these cities compared with Vienna? he said. We hate
Vienna, and yet we love it like no other city. Just as we
hate the Burgtheater, though we love it like no other theater.
This success I've had with Ekdal was quite unpredictable,
he said, and as he said this I was watching Jeannie Billroth,
who had become somewhat agitated, feeling that this evening she had been pushed into the background; she could
not make herself the focus of attention that she always
wanted to be, since the Burgtheater actor had so far not
allowed her to get a word in, despite her repeated attempts
to intervene. Again and again she had tried to take him up

on some remark or other, but he had not given her the chance. But now, having heard him say that Ekdal was the most difficult part he had ever studied or played, she managed to remark that in her opinion the role of Edgar in Strindberg was much more difficult. *But Edgar is a much more difficult part than Ekdal,* she said. At any rate that had always been her impression from reading the play. She had never thought of Ekdal as a difficult part—except of course that all parts are difficult if they are to be well played and if they actually are well played. She had always felt, when reading the plays, that Edgar was more difficult than Ekdal. *No!* cried the Burgtheater actor, *Ekdal is the more difficult of the two—that's obvious.* There she could not agree with him, said Jeannie Billroth, pointing out that she had once studied drama, *incidentally under the famous Professor Kindermann.* This evening too, as on all such occasions, she managed to mention the fact that she was once a pupil of Kindermann. Perhaps an actor was bound to think that Ekdal was the more difficult part, she said, whereas in fact Edgar was the more difficult. No, you must understand, the actor said to Jeannie Billroth, that when one has been an actor for decades, as I have—and an actor at the Burgtheater moreover—and when one has played nothing but leading roles for as long as one cares to think back, one knows what one is talking about. As a student of drama, of course, one has quite different views about the theater, he went on, but there's no doubt that Ekdal is the more difficult role and Edgar the easier— easier when it comes to playing it, don't forget. Jeannie Billroth was not satisfied with what the actor had said, and replied that it had surely been a proven fact for as long as the two roles had existed that Ekdal, not Edgar, was the easier role to play. Kindermann, her teacher, had demonstrated this quite clearly in an article entitled *Edgar and Ekdal: A Comparison.* Had he not read the article? Jeannie Billroth asked, to which he replied that he was not familiar with Kindermann's article. That was regrettable, said Jeannie Billroth, for if he had read Kindermann's discussion of Edgar (a Strindberg character) and Ekdal (an Ibsen character) before beginning rehearsals he could have spared himself *many of the unpleasant aspects* of his study of *The Wild Duck,* whereupon Auersberger, who had been on the look-out for an opportunity to say something himself, suddenly interjected, *And all those weeks in the chalet!* By now the actor himself wanted to change the subject and announced that he had lost one of his gloves on the way to the Gentzgasse. Had he not been late setting out he would have gone back to look for it, but he could not retrace his steps as he did not want to keep the Auersbergers *on the rack* any longer. People did not know what they were letting themselves in for when they invited him to dinner. It's easy enough to invite me, he said, but the hosts don't realize what's involved until they notice that it's half past twelve and the guest still hasn't arrived. *Yes, acting is quite a profession,* he said, as though this were one of the remarks he habitually made when he was at a loss for anything else to say. The hostess, who had had a second serving of pike brought to the table, remarked that it really was a pity he had lost one of his gloves on the way to the Gentzgasse. Losing *one* glove was just as bad as losing two, she said, as there was nothing one could do with one glove. And all the people at the table said that they had once lost a single glove and had the same feeling. But possibly whoever had found the glove would have handed it in, the hostess suggested. *Where would he have handed it in?* Auersberger asked his wife, with a burst of laughter which prompted everybody else to laugh. Who might have handed the glove in or might still do so, and where? he asked. Whereupon everyone sitting around the table re-counted his *own* glove story. It transpired that they had all lost one glove on some occasion and felt the loss of one as keenly as the loss of a pair. And none of them had found the lost glove—none of the gloves had been handed in. Oh, if only it had been a pair! Auersberger's wife said, and proceeded to tell her own glove story. About twenty years ago she had gone to the ladies' room at the Josefstadt Theater and left her black evening gloves there. *Both of them*, she said, looking around at the assembled company. The play was *Der Zerrissene*, one of Nestroy's best, she added. She had left her gloves in the ladies' room during the interval, and immediately after the performance she had gone back to get them, assuming that they would still be on the table where she had left them. *In the Josefstadt I naturally took it for granted*, she said, *that my gloves would still be there. But they'd gone*. The attendant knew nothing about them, she said. But just imagine: two weeks after the performance of *Der Zerrissene* my evening gloves were returned to me. Anonymously, she added, leaning back in her chair for a moment—anonymously, and ac-companied by a little card with the words *Best wishes* written on it. To this day I don't know who it was who returned my evening gloves, she said. Shortly after this the actor turned to her and said: *An excellent pike, a genuine Balaton pike*, and the others indicated that they too had the same impression—that the pike they were eating was indeed a genuine Balaton pike. But you know, said the actor, who every now and then used his napkin, which he had stuck in his shirt collar, to wipe his mouth and surrounding beard, acting is quite a profession. Once, ages ago, when I was playing in Munich—*at short notice, as they say*—in the role of Heinrich (though that's beside the point), I met a colleague in the Kaufingerstrasse whom I'd known some time earlier, before the war, and whom I'd shared digs with in the Lerchenfelderstrasse. No heating, as you may imagine, rats all over the place, nothing to eat—you know what it was like at the time: the Americans hadn't arrived and the Russians were already there. Anyhow, I asked this colleague why he'd left Vienna. I'll tell you why, he said: I'm utterly sick of Vienna. And what about Munich? I asked him, the Burgtheater actor went on, wiping his bearded chin. And he said, I'm utterly sick of Munich as well! So you might just as well have stayed in Vienna, I said, if you're sick of Munich too. Incidentally this colleague was engaged at the time to play the kind of roles I played, the actor went on. Possibly his voice was too high-pitched for the roles he was called upon to play. It was a Strindberg voice, not an Ibsen voice. Fine for Goethe, but not for Shakespeare—and no good at all for Ibsen. All right for Molière, but not for Nestroy, certainly not for Nestroy, he said. Perhaps he was too fat—an undisciplined life-style, said the actor from the Burgtheater. Born at Vöcklabruck, basically a provincial, but a nice enough fellow—voice too high-pitched, married young, one child, divorced, long engagement at the Volkstheater. So you might just as well have stayed in Vienna, I said to him. He had a curious facial twitch, the actor recalled—a man with a great sense of humor, but he always got through all his money—an easygoing type, very easygoing. I told him I was rehearsing the role of Edgar. Oh, Edgar, he said—I'm not interested. Not interested? I said. Not interested? It was so cold, and I hadn't any gloves—I was freezing the whole time. I'm rehearsing the role of Edgar,

I repeated, but he wasn't listening. I'm rehearsing Edgar! I shouted at him, the actor recalled. Then I turned on my heel and left him. A sweet man, the actor said, helping himself to a spoonful of caper sauce. Next day I read in the evening paper that he'd killed himself. In the Kaufinger-strasse, where he was living, though I didn't know he was living there. *Hanged himself!* the Burgtheater actor said, drawing out the syllables. Actors are predestined to kill themselves, to hang themselves, said the actor from the Burgtheater. I'm not the suicidal type—not at all—but when I think of how many people in my line of business have killed themselves! Thoroughly talented people, the actor said, *all of them potentially great actors,* and they go and kill themselves. I was the last person to speak to him. We'd known each other since we were young. All the best people kill themselves, he said, taking a gulp of wine. The weather has a great deal to do with suicide, he said. The Burgtheater actor, having become somewhat melancholy through telling the story about the actor who had committed suicide in Munich, now recalled that Joana, whom he had not known personally, but whom the rest of us had known, had killed herself a few days earlier and been buried only that afternoon at Kilb. I assume that he had learned this from Auersberger. *I once saw your friend Joana when she gave a talk at the Burgtheater about the art of movement, as she called it.* I remember her very clearly, he said, suddenly affecting an attitude of grief and modulating his voice into a mourning key. A gifted person, he said, but quite out of place at the Burgtheater. The course she gave was an unfortunate mistake, he said. He then went on to say that during the past year he had at-tended the funerals of several fellow actors—there had been *an unprecedented number of deaths among actors,* he said, adding, *and among cabaret artists*. Ah yes, he said, addressing Jeannie Billroth, I know what it means to lose a lifelong friend. But when we reach a certain age we lose all the people who mean anything to us, all the people we love. He took a gulp of wine, and the hostess filled up his glass. So long as it's a quick death, he said. Nothing is more dreadful than a protracted illness. It's a blessing when somebody just collapses and dies, he said. But I'm not the suicidal type, he said again. There were more women who killed themselves than men, he said. Whereupon Jeannie Billroth pointed out that this was not true: statistics showed that the number of male suicides was double the number of female suicides. Suicide is a male problem, she said. She had read a study of the incidence of suicide in Austria, which showed that, *as a percentage of the total population*, as she put it, more people killed themselves in Austria than in any other country in Europe. Hungary had the second highest suicide rate and Sweden the third highest. And in Austria, interestingly enough, the people most likely to commit suicide were those who lived in the Salzburg region, in other words the most beautiful part of Austria. *The Styrians are rather prone to suicide*, said Auersberger, who by this stage was just about totally drunk and had become highly agitated. He told the actor that he was surprised that so few Burgtheater actors killed themselves, since they had such good reason to do so. Saying this he burst out laughing at his own remark, though the others merely found it embarrassing and glared at him. I myself momentarily joined in his laughter, thinking that despite his generally repugnant behavior Auersberger had a certain clownish wit that occasionally made even me laugh, averse though I generally am to jokes. What do you mean? the actor asked. I mean something quite simple, Auersberger replied: if the actors at the Burgtheater realized how pathetic their acting was, they'd all have to kill themselves. Present company excepted, Auersberger added, draining his glass. All right, the Burgtheater actor replied, if that's what you think of the Burgtheater, why do you still go? Auersberger replied that he had not been to the Burgtheater for ten years. His wife at once corrected him, saying that only two weeks ago they had seen the performance of *Der Verschwender. Oh yes, Der Verschwender*, Auersberger retorted, *and the performance was so bad that it turned my stomach, and I immediately forgot all about it.* At first the actor did not know how to react to Auersberger's remarks. The Burgtheater has always had its detractors, he said, which is what happens to any institution that is superlatively good. The Burgtheater has always been attacked, especially by those who have been eager to join it and been rejected. All the actors who haven't had an engagement with the Burgtheater, he said, inveigh against it until they land one. It's always been like that. Anything out of the ordinary attracts hostility, he said. Hating the Burgtheater is an old Viennese tradition, just like hating the State Opera. Even the theater managers hate the Burgtheater, constantly ridiculing it until they succeed, by their unscrupulous endeavors, in becoming Burgtheater managers themselves. But look, the actor continued: where else would you see a performance of *The Wild Duck* like the one we're doing at the Burgtheater? Nowhere! You can go wherever you like, but nowhere will you find a comparable performance of *The Wild Duck*. Nowhere, Auersberger replied, since you've just said yourself that this production of *The Wild Duck* at the Burgtheater is a failure, and that according to the critics the only successful aspect of the production is your own performance in the role of Ekdal. Your performance as Ekdal is superb, but apart from that the production's no good. You can't put it like that, the actor said, you can't say that this production of *The Wild Duck* is no good, even though it may have its shortcomings. Even this partial failure is *much preferable to all the other Wild Ducks I've ever seen, and I've seen all the Wild Ducks that have been put on in recent years.* I once saw *The Wild Duck* in Berlin, *the first postwar Wild Duck*, the Burgtheater actor said, at the *Freie Volksbühne*; I also saw *The Wild Duck* at the *Schillertheater*. Both of them disastrous productions—and the same was true in Munich and Stuttgart. The German theater is praised only by total incompetents who haven't the first notion of what theater is all about. *It's all fashionable journalism written by half-baked critics*, said the actor. No, no, this *Wild Duck* at the Burgtheater is the best *Wild Duck* I've ever seen, and I'm not speaking from prejudice, even though I'm playing Ekdal in it. It's far and away the best *Wild Duck*. I once saw the play in Stockholm—in Swedish the title is *Vildanden*. I didn't like it at all. I felt I had to go to Stockholm *to see the best Wild Duck there was to be seen*, but it was a total disappointment. It's not true that Scandinavian theaters put on the best performances of Scandinavian plays. I once saw a performance of *The Wild Duck* in Augsburg and found it far superior to anything I'd seen in Scandinavia. Naturally everything depends on Ekdal. If Ekdal's no good the whole play's no good. Don't imagine for one moment that you hear the best Mozart performances in Salzburg or Vienna. People always make the mistake of thinking that a play gets its best productions in its country of origin. But they're quite wrong. I once saw a Molière play performed in Hamburg in a way you'd never see it performed in Paris. And a Shakespeare production in Cologne that put all English Shakespeare productions in the shade. Of course it's only in Vienna that you can see a good Nestroy production, the actor added. *But not at the Burgtheater,* Auersberger interjected. *You're probably right there,* replied the actor. *I have to admit that you've got a point. There's never been a successful Nestroy production at the Burgtheater. But then where has there ever been a successful Nestroy production? Surely not at the Volkstheater, where by rights he belongs? Of course not at the Volkstheater,* Auersberger replied—*at the Karltheater, but that was pulled down nearly thirty years ago.* Yes, said the actor, it's a great pity the Karltheater was demolished. In a way, he observed not unwittily, when they demolished the Karltheater they also demolished Nestroy. By *they* he meant the Viennese authorities, who have most of the city's demolished theaters on their conscience. After the war more than half the theaters in Vienna were torn down, said Auersberger. Alas, how right you are! said the actor. In Vienna it's always the best that gets demolished, Auersberger continued; the Viennese always demolish the best, but at the time they don't realize that it's the best—that dawns on them only after the event. The Viennese as a whole are expert demolishers and destroyers, demolition and destruction specialists. How right you are! said the actor, who had by now finished eating and had his glass replenished by the hostess. If a building in Vienna is especially beautiful, he went on, it's sure to be demolished sooner or later—no matter whether it's a particularly beautiful building or a particularly successful institution, the Viennese don't rest content until it's been demolished. And they treat people in just the same way, the actor went on: being incapable of recognizing a person's goodness or worth, they proceed to tear him down, just as they would tear down a monument, having suddenly forgotten that it was they who put it up in the first place. *My interpretation of Ekdal is in a certain sense philosophical*, said the actor, *but when you read what's been written about Ibsen you're none the wiser—on the contrary, you find that it only deranges the mind. And you can't approach an exacting role like Ekdal with your mind deranged*, said the actor. Young Werle, Gregers—that would have been the part for me thirty years ago, perhaps even twenty years ago. I'd have liked to play it, but whenever I got anywhere near playing it, *The Wild Duck* was taken off the repertory. Gregers would have been an even more appropriate part for me to play, he said, looking around at the others. I had the impression that none of them knew what he was talking about, except for Jeannie Billroth, who had just admitted to having recently read and seen *The Wild Duck* for the first time. Gregers would really have been the part for me, rather than Ekdal, said the actor, and it was now clear that nobody at the table knew what he meant. I used to dream of playing Gregers, he said. I was once invited to play the part in Düsseldorf, but I turned the invitation down because I didn't want to leave Vienna. If I'd gone to Düsseldorf to play Gregers—who knows?—I might have lost my contract with the Burgtheater. I was naturally thankful to be engaged by the Burgtheater, he said, but all my life it's pained me to have forfeited the chance to play Gregers. Only once was I offered the part. I always thought I'd play it one day, but I never did. If we pass up a chance like that, he said, it never comes around again. *Psychological theater*, said the actor, leaning back in his chair after accepting a cigar from Auersberger's wife. She made to light it for him, but he forestalled her and lit it himself. We always want the highest, he said, but we don't attain the highest just by wanting it, he said, uttering this sentence as though it were a quotation, possibly from some play or other. While he was having such a success as Ekdal, he said, he was already preparing for his next role. In an English play, he said. An English director was coming over from London, and rehearsals were due to start the following week. An English conversation piece, but not Oscar Wilde, he said. Oh no! And naturally not Shaw. *Something contemporary!* he exclaimed, *something contemporary!* Amusing, but profound! Set in a theatrical milieu incidentally. He played the part of a writer who had married into the aristocracy. Not necessarily first class, he said, but entertaining and not unintelligent, far from unintelligent in fact—a very English play, good entertainment value and not excessively demanding intellectually. A rather sloppy translation, he said, but I'm tidying up the text. *If only we had one good writer!* he suddenly exclaimed, *but we haven't any.* In the whole of Germany there isn't a single good writer, let alone in Austria—to say nothing of Switzerland. And as a result only foreign plays are put on—plays by English, French or Polish playwrights. It's a calamity, he lamented. Not a single readable play in twenty years. Dramatic talent has died out in German-speaking Europe, he said, leaning back and blowing his cigar smoke at Auersberger, who promptly began to cough. Probably the age we live in isn't an age for playwrights, said the actor. When a talent does emerge it soon turns out to be a non-talent. How much garbage gets rave notices in the press! he said. It's incredible what passes for talent these days, what is regarded as dramatic art. I found myself sickened by what he was saying. You know, he went on, you've no idea what it's like having to rehearse with untalented people, having to grind away with them for weeks, sometimes for months. Young people in the theater today are all so spoiled, he said; the papers are always saying that they're so gifted, that they're geniuses, while in reality they've no gift whatever, not the least talent. And their most notable characteristic is their indolence. Like the rest of today's youth they're thoroughly *spoiled, having been brought up in the most stupid fashion,* said the actor. While I was working on *The Wild Duck* I saw what was wrong with these young people: they will not tolerate discipline. But the actor who plays Gregers is quite outstanding, Jeannie Billroth objected at this point. To which the Burgtheater actor replied, Everybody says Gregers is good, but I don't understand what they see in him: I find his performance just average, no more than average—a piece of positive miscasting. Jeannie Billroth was the only other guest who had actually seen the production at the Burgtheater, and the others, having started off without even knowing what *The Wild Duck* was and only gradually learning that it was a play, were condemned to silence. Every now and then they nodded, either looking straight at the actor or gazing down at the tablecloth, or else staring in bewilderment at the person sitting opposite; they had no chance whatever of participating in the actor's performance, with which he was regaling them so uninhibitedly, knowing that none of them could inhibit him. Auersberger's wife, far from inhibiting him, repeatedly urged him to go on, and it was natural that the actor, having just come from performing in *The Wild Duck* at the Burgtheater, should continue to expatiate on the performance and related matters. It was a wonder, he said, that *The Wild Duck* had been put on at all in Vienna—*put on* was a phrase he used repeatedly—since putting it on in Vienna was *a risk*. After all *The*

Wild Duck was *a modern play*. He actually used the term modern to describe a play that was just a hundred years old and was still as great, after a hundred years, as it was when it was written: to call such a play modern was patent nonsense. To present *The Wild Duck* to the Viennese public was not just a *risk*, said the actor, but *a considerable gamble*. The Viennese simply *did not respond to modern drama*, as he put it—they never had responded to modern drama. They preferred to go and see classical plays, and *The Wild Duck* was not a classical play—it was a modern play, which might admittedly one day *become* a classic. Ibsen might one day join the classics, and so might Strindberg, said the actor. He had often felt that Strindberg was a greater dramatist than Ibsen. Yet at other times, he said, I've felt the opposite to be true—that Ibsen is superior to Strindberg and has a better prospect of becoming a classic. Sometimes I think *Miss Julie* will one day become a classic, and at other times I think it'll be a play like *The Wild Duck*. But if we attach too much importance to Strindberg we do Ibsen an injustice, he said, just as we do Strindberg an injustice if we attach too much importance to Ibsen. Personally, he said, he loved *the Nordic way of writing, the Nordic way of writing for the theater*. He had always loved Edvard Munch too. *I've always loved The Cry*, he said—*which of course you are all familiar with. What an extraordinary work of art!* I once went to Oslo just to see *The Cry*, when it was still in Oslo. That doesn't mean that I have a preference for the Scandinavian countries, he said. Whenever I was in Scandinavia I had a nostalgia for the south, or at least for Germany, he said. Stockholm—what a dreary city! To say nothing of Oslo—so enervating, so soul-destroying. And Copenhagen—enough said! Young actors are always clamoring to get to the Burgtheater, he said, and even if they have no talent they get engagements there through personal connections—through having an uncle who's on the board of management of the Volksoper or an official of the Federal Theater Trust. If somebody has an aunt in the Ministry of Education, he's taken on at the Burgtheater as soon as he's qualified at the Reinhardt Seminar, said the actor, though he may not have the slightest talent. These twenty-year-olds then sit around in the rehearsal rooms, blocking the way for other people and simply making a nuisance of themselves. *Semi-talents at best*, said the actor, which simply atrophy in our leading theater, keeping out the genuine talents. The only advice I would give to a young person with genuine talent would be not to go to the Burgtheater, since that would be a sure path to total destruction at the very beginning of his development, said the actor, helping himself to the dessert, a rum-flavored chocolate cake covered in whipped cream, of which I ate only one mouthful, reflecting that a dessert like that was far too rich for such a late supper. But all the others ate theirs, and so did the actor from the Burgtheater, who, having eaten half of his dessert, returned to the subject of *The Wild Duck*. Actually I should have played in *Wallenstein*, and originally I was to have played in the new Calderón production, but nothing came of either, I'm now thankful to say. I myself never dreamed of such a success, *such a resounding success*, said the actor. To think that *The Wild Duck* was produced at the Burgtheater— and was a success! He had been *completely bowled over*, he said. In April I'm going on my annual journey to Spain, he said—Andalusia, Seville, Granada, Ronda, he said, finishing his dessert. *My Spanish nostalgia*, he said, his mouth still full of chocolate cake. It was almost impossible to follow what he was saying with his mouth full of chocolate cake, even when, alarmed at his own table manners, he said, I do beg your pardon! and gulped down the last mouthful. In recent years I've taken to visiting Spain, turning my back on Italy so to speak. Spain is still an unspoiled country—at least large parts of it are unspoiled—so *sparse*, he said, using his napkin to wipe not only his mouth and mustache, but the whole of his beard and his forehead. Charles V, the Prado, he said, looking around the table. *Of course I'm no connoisseur of art*, he said, *just an art lover—that's the difference*. But when I think of Italy I feel sick, he said, whereas the thought of Spain really excites me. In Italy more or less everything screams to high heaven, but in Spain you still have this historical sparseness, this historical tranquillity, if you see what I mean. It's no bad thing for an actor to make a longish journey once a year. It doesn't have to be to Africa or the Caribbean. In my case it's Spain, especially La Mancha—I find it regenerating. And believe it or not, I have a passion for bullfighting. *An affinity with Hemingway*, he said, *a real affinity with Hemingway*. But I'm not such a romantic as Hemingway was—more a man of reason, said the Burgtheater actor. I don't have the romantic American view of bullfighting—I have a more scientific approach. Whatever is profound is naturally unromantic, he said. Nothing profound is romantic. Indeed, he said suddenly, suicide is a fashionable contemporary sickness. Now *I* am not the suicidal type. *Joana—a Spanish name*, he said. Twice he said *Joana—a Spanish name*, then leaned back and asked Auersberger whether his latest cantata had been published. *All your cantatas are in print, aren't they?* he asked. Auersberger said, *Yes, my latest cantata is in print*. And is it going to be performed in Vienna? asked the actor. *I doubt it*, replied the successor of Webern. It would be impossible, he explained, to find first-class performers

for his *complicated cantata in Vienna. At either the Konzerthaus or the Musikverein*, said Webern's successor, raising his head to its full height. *There's not one flautist in
the whole of Austria who could play it*, said Auersberger.
But I hear the London performance was very good, said
the actor. *Yes*, replied Auersberger, the successor of Webern,
London was the only place where his cantata could be
performed as he envisaged it, where it could be performed
ideally. His wife at once joined in, echoing the word *ideally*,
after which they both repeated the word several times, so
that it seemed as though *everybody* was saying *ideally*—
everybody except Jeannie Billroth, who had sat watching
me, consumed with hatred, all the time the actor was
talking. It was now impossible to imagine that thirty years
ago, even twenty-five years ago, I had read poems by
Eluard to her while sitting on her sofa and stroking the
soles of her feet, that I had played short scenes from Molière
for her in her bedroom while she sat virtually naked on the
bed, repeatedly demanding that I play these scenes from
Molière after I had obviously bored her with my readings
from Joyce and Valéry. It was inconceivable now that I
had once read her the letters that her friend Ernstl wrote
to her from the Salzkammergut. She wanted no one but
me to read her these letters, which she described as *the
most intimate letters imaginable*—which indeed they were,
as I now recalled—while *she devoured me with her gaze*,
as they say. That I used to spend hours reading the text of
one of her novels to her, thus affording her hours of supreme
gratification while I myself became more and more depressed, and that I was the one who thought up a title for
this novel, *The Wilderness of Youth*, under which title it
subsequently appeared—regrettably, I thought. That I used
to walk for hours with her in the Prater, once even going

up on the Giant Wheel with her, talking to her all the while about Pavese, Ungaretti and Pirandello, that I had been to Kagran and Kaisermühlen with her on a number of occasions, because when I was with her I always felt an urge to cross over the Reichsbrücke to the north bank of the Danube, I thought. That she was *the first artistic person* I met in Vienna after completing my studies in Salzburg, I thought. That *she* was the first person in Vienna who heard me read *my* poems and did not immediately reject them as worthless—which was what had always happened back home—and hence the first person, as I now recalled, who can be said to have given me literary courage, for whatever reason. To think that I once loved this woman Jeannie Billroth, whom I have hated for the last twenty years, and who, also, hates me. People come together and form a friendship, and for years they not only endure this friendship, but allow it to become more and more intense until it finally snaps, and from then on they hate each other for decades, sometimes for the rest of their lives. For years I used to go and visit Jeannie Billroth, I thought. At this point the actor suddenly started recounting anecdotes, the kind of theatrical anecdotes that always go down well in Vienna and provide life support for many a Viennese party that would otherwise be in danger of dying of paralysis. Most Viennese parties are able to survive for a few evening hours only because these theatrical anecdotes are continually dished up, and this party in the Gentzgasse, which has been officially designated an *artistic dinner party*, is no exception, I thought. It was through Jeannie Billroth that I met the Auersbergers, and finally Joana, I thought. I met Jeannie through a philosopher friend of my grandfather's whom I visited in the Maxinggasse in Hietzing thirty years ago at a time when I was extremely hard up and on the verge of starvation. It was my visit to the Maxinggasse in Hietzing that saved my life, I told myself—to the so-called Johann Strauss House, which was occupied by my grandfather's philosopher friend, whose brother played the bassoon and the horn in the Vienna Philharmonic. I now recalled how, having arrived in Vienna without a penny and being close to starvation, even to suicide, I had summoned up what little strength I still had and made my way to the Maxinggasse, to an address that my grandfather had given me, hoping that I would somehow be saved. And the Maxinggasse did save me. First I was given a drink of milk, then something to eat, and finally a recommendation to a woman writer who lived on the west bank of the river Wien, by the chain bridge. She got me to clear out her cellar, and for this she paid me enough money to keep me above water for three days. I read a few of her poems at the time, and these made a considerable impact on me. It was through this writer, who died young, that I met Jeannie Billroth. I now recalled how Jeannie and I used to visit Joana at Kilb, and how we would often go to the *Iron Hand* with her and Fritz to eat and drink and play cards. It was after all Jeannie who introduced me to nearly all the great writers of the twentieth century by lending me copies of their works. That was the Jeannie of those days, I thought, not the Jeannie who was now sitting opposite me, filled with hatred because I escaped from her one day rather than let myself be devoured by her. Had I not escaped from her, at the high point in our relationship so to speak, I would inevitably have been devoured and annihilated. So I suddenly stopped visiting her. She waited in vain for me to appear. While Ernstl was working at his *Chemical Institute*, I had spent hundreds of afternoons with her behind drawn curtains, as I now recalled, either reading the great works of the major twentieth-century writers to her, or listening to her as she read them to me. And then, when Ernstl came home, we would all have a *cold supper*, or a goulash that had been warmed up a second time and so tasted outstandingly good. And when Ernstl was tired and had gone to bed, she would make me read Joyce or Saint-John Perse or Virginia Woolf to her again until I was quite exhausted, I now recalled. I never left Jeannie's until about two o'clock in the morning, when I would set off home to Währing, walking down the Radetzkystrasse and along by the Danube Canal, my mind brimming with world literature. We stick to someone for years, I thought, looking straight at Jeannie; we are fascinated by them and in the end become utterly dependent on them, not only head over heels in love, as they say, but utterly in thrall, and when we leave them we believe we are finished, as I did at the time, yet one day we stop going to see them, without giving any reason. Not only do we stop visiting them—we *shun* them, we start to despise and hate them, and no longer want to see them. And then we do see them, and we fall prey to a terrible agitation that we can't control. All the other people I met at the funeral in Kilb meant virtually nothing to me, I now thought, even the Auersbergers, but meeting Jeannie instantly plunged me into mental turmoil. I had thought of them all on the way to Kilb, all except Jeannie, and naturally I had not considered *the dreadful possibility of meeting her again*. But there she was. She even shook hands with me at the cemetery—she even managed to smile at me, I recalled, but it was an almost *annihilating* smile. Yet perhaps I returned it with an equally annihilating smile. I hated her as she stood by the open grave, acting the part of the lifelong friend, I now thought, going closer to the grave than anyone else, taking a handful of earth from the sexton's shovel and throwing it into the grave with a dexterous movement of the hand. I must stop going to her apartment before she kills me, I had thought almost thirty years ago, and I had simply *made good my escape*, one might say. My behavior was not as despicable as might be thought: I acted in self-defense, fearful for my own survival, I now told myself, providing myself with an excuse that I could not expect anyone else to provide and did not demand from anyone. We meet someone at the right moment, I thought, we take everything we need from them, and then we leave them, again at the right moment. I met Jeannie Billroth at just the right moment and left her at the right moment—just as I've always left everybody at the right moment, it now occurred to me. We adapt ourselves to the mentality and temperament of a person like Jeannie, and for a time we take in only what this person's mentality and temperament have to offer us, and when we think we've taken in enough—when we've had enough—we simply sever the connection, just as I severed my connection with Jeannie. We spend years sucking all we can out of someone, and then, having almost sucked them dry, we suddenly say that we ourselves are being sucked dry. And for the rest of our lives we have to live with the knowledge of our own baseness, I now reflected. And having parted from Jeannie, I *changed sides* and went over to the Auersbergers *with colors flying*, as it were—and to Joana. I had broken with Jeannie, to whom I owed almost everything at that time—simply deserting her for the Auersbergers and Joana, attaching myself for two or three years first to the Auersbergers, by whom I was immediately fascinated, and then to Joana. For the fact is that the moment I deserted the Auersbergers, the moment I escaped from them, one might say, I flung myself at Joana; having given up the Gentzgasse and Maria Zaal, at first inwardly and then outwardly, I opted for the Sebastiansplatz. After Jeannie had initiated me into the literature of the twentieth century and the Auersbergers had enabled me to widen my knowledge to an unbelievable extent—when suddenly the art of literature, especially twentieth-century literature, was no longer a mystery to me, thanks to Jeannie and the Auersbergers, I fell upon the so-called *plastic arts*; from now on all my interest was directed to these and to *acting*—and of course to *the art of movement*, to *dance*, and to *choreography*, since it was only here that Joana was truly in her element. Looking back, I now thought as I sat facing Jeannie, I chose what was for me an *ideal course of development*. I chose this development, I thought—I did not think: I underwent this development, which proved to be absolutely ideal—I thought: I *chose* this ideal development for myself, I chose what was for me the ideal artistic development. This idea gave me pleasure—above all, I think, because all at once the notion of *artistic development* seemed self-evident. There could have been no more ideal, no more logical development for me, I now thought—encountering first Jeannie Billroth the writer, then the Auersbergers, and finally Joana—and through Jeannie her *chemical friend Ernstl*, and through Joana her tapestry artist Fritz; I could not have made a happier choice. Yet now I hated Jeannie, who was sitting opposite me, and she hated me. This hatred would of course be susceptible of precise analysis, but I have no wish to analyze it, though possibly Jeannie made her own analysis long ago. And a person like this ends up writing worthless sentimental prose, and poems that are equally worthless and sentimental, and finally falls into the universal cesspit of petit bourgeois mediocrity, I thought. We respect somebody—we may respect them for years—and then suddenly come to hate them, without at first knowing *why*. And we find it quite intolerable that this person, whom for so long we respected and perhaps even loved, who as it were opened our eyes and ears to everything, who revealed the whole world to us, and above all the world of art—that a person like this, who for so many years preached the *highest standards*, *supreme standards*, who guided and educated us to these supreme standards, should have ended up producing such miserable art and cultivating such appalling dilettantism. We simply cannot understand how such a person can eventually have produced something worthless and repellent, I now thought, and we can't forgive them because, by merely pretending to subscribe to these supreme standards, they have cheated and deceived us. Jeannie cheated and deceived you with her own dilettantism, I told myself as I watched her sitting there, filled with hatred and revulsion and having to endure the actor's endless anecdotes. Like all the others, he was leaning back in his chair, no doubt expecting that the Auersbergers would shortly ask the by-now stiff and lifeless company around the dinner table to get up and repair to the music room. I find nothing more distasteful than listening to the Viennese recounting their anecdotes, and I have to endure this Viennese perversion too, I thought. The Auersbergers' dining room suddenly reminded me of a chapel of rest, largely no doubt because they had meanwhile switched off all the electric lights, so that the room was now lit only by the candles in the Empire lamps on the dining table. One could now see only the contours of the furniture in the dining room; one could no longer see the perverse beauty of the room— which I used to think altogether too beautiful—but only its somber theatricality. This atmosphere was in tune with the present company, who were waiting for a signal from the hosts that they might leave the dining room and move to the greater comfort of the music room. They seemed to have been plunged into a mood of despondency, above all by Joana's death, but also by the lateness of the hour, I thought, and not even the actor was disposed to go on talking. He loosened his tie and undid the top button of his shirt, murmuring something about fresh air, whereupon the hostess jumped up to open a window. She opened the window overlooking the courtyard, rather than the one that gave onto the street, expecting the air to be fresher from that quarter. After this she went out into the music room, then returned to the dining room and sat down again at the table. She could have believed anything of Joana, she said, resuming her place at the table, but not that she would kill herself. The actor again brought up the case of his colleague who went to Munich, whom he described as *an unhappy man right from the start.* All these suicides, he said, were unhappy people right from the start, sometimes more so, sometimes less, but always essentially unhappy. It never comes as a surprise when they end up killing themselves, he said. When Joana was engaged by the Burgtheater management to teach the actors how to walk he had found the whole idea crazy. The managers of the Burgtheater were forever coming up with crazy ideas, he said. They wanted to help people like Joana, but this meant that they were bound to come up with some crazy idea. The actors at the Burgtheater are quite capable of walking, he said, and of standing and sitting and lying. He could clearly remember the observations of one Viennese criticaster, as he put it, which were published in the *Presse*, to the effect that the actors at the Burgtheater *could neither walk nor speak*, or at least that they *could not do both at once.* Whenever a critic writes this kind of nonsense, said the actor, it's immediately taken up by the theater management. In this case they engaged a *speech instructor*, so that the actors could learn to speak. Absurd! said the actor. But if it helped our dear departed friend, he said, then there was some point in it. While he was speaking I recalled how distastefully Jeannie had behaved at Kilb. After the funeral she had gone to the woman from the general store and pressed a hundred-schilling note into her hand to cover the cost of the telephone call she had made from Kilb to inform her of Joana's death. Less than a hundred yards from the grave she had pressed this hundred-schilling note into the woman's hand, I thought, in such a tasteless manner that the woman could not help feeling insulted. In fact she really was insulted by Jeannie's behavior, for it would never occur to a person like her to expect to be reimbursed for making a telephone call to report her friend's death to another friend. But Jeannie always went in for that kind of tasteless behavior, I thought: she hasn't changed. But not content with this, she turned up at the *Iron Hand*, where I had gone with the woman from the general store to continue our conversation about Joana, and had the impertinence to go around among the funeral guests begging for money for *poor John*, who was now *all alone*, she said, and *had to pay* for all the funeral arrangements—who did not have a single penny, but had to meet all the expenses connected with Joana's funeral. She would make the *first donation*, as she put it, by contributing five hundred schillings. Jeannie has always played the Good Samaritan, I now reflected, and I've always found it repugnant, since she's never been motivated by genuine charity: it's always been an act intended to demonstrate her social concern. All her life she's had an unstable and unsavory character and has never been above using any available means to put others in the wrong, as she did at Kilb after Joana's funeral. She had the *audacity* to pick up an empty cigar box and place her own five-hundred-schilling note in it, then go from one mourner to another canvassing contributions, with an expression on her face that made one want to slap it rather than give her any money for John, poor though he may have been—holding out the cigar box and carefully noting the amounts her victims were prepared to contribute and actually did contribute. Everyone found this performance of hers quite tasteless, and curiously enough it was Auersberger who voiced their feelings by suddenly saying to her face, *How tasteless you are, how tasteless, how tasteless!* Twice he repeated the words *how tasteless*—in other words he uttered them three times altogether—and then threw a thousand-schilling note into the cigar box. Finally there was a sum of several thousand schillings in the box, together with a hundred and twenty pounds which I had put in. Jeannie walked over to the table at which John was sitting with the woman from the store and myself and tipped out the contents of the cigar box on the table in front of him, behaving as though it were *her* money, *all her own work*, as it were. And indeed it was *all her own tasteless work*, but by no means her own money—her own tastelessness, but not her own money, I had said to myself at the time, though I refrained from telling her that I thought she was *disgusting*. That was the proper word for her, and it was on the tip of my tongue. The Virginia Woolf of Vienna, I thought at the time, who has used John as a means of once more parading her social concern, thereby facing him with one of the most embarrassing situations of his life! He would have liked to crawl under the table. People like Jeannie

Billroth, who have a great understanding of art (or used to have), lack any instinct for real life, for dealing with real people, I thought. And this, it now occurred to me, has more than a little to do with the fact that, having perhaps once been a truly gifted artist, an artist of considerable talent, Jeannie has in the course of the last two decades developed into an unscrupulous, petit bourgeois hypocrite of the most dreadful kind. But she always made this hypocritical pretense to social concern, I thought, though thirty years ago, even twenty years ago, this repellent side of her character did not strike me with such depressing force as it does today, I thought. In fact in those days I was unaware of her weaknesses and the generally disagreeable traits in her personality. For a long time we see only one side of a person's personality, because for reasons of self-preservation we do not wish to see any other, I thought, then suddenly we see all sides of their personality and are disgusted by them, I thought. I sat in the *Iron Hand* for over two hours, and finally took my leave shortly after Jeannie had left for Vienna with the Auersbergers. Once more I could see her ostentatious fir wreath adorned with a bright silvery bow imprinted with the words *From Jeannie*, which the sexton had contrived to place on top of the pile of flowers by the graveside in such a way that everybody saw only the one name *Jeannie*. Not that I suspect Jeannie of having prevailed upon the sexton to give her wreath such prominence, but all the same it was *her* wreath with the words *From Jeannie* that had pride of place, and this seemed to sum up the whole of her performance at Kilb. She was also the only one who had prayed aloud with the local people; this I found almost insufferable, considering that Jeannie is not a Catholic and has always disparaged Christianity, at least when speaking to me. She put on a show of being pious, and this was the most repulsive aspect of the ceremony; no one else, I thought, had made this distasteful pretense of piety. At Kilb she behaved altogether as though she were *Joana's best friend*, though I know that in reality she had let Joana down, abandoning her at the very moment when she was deserted by Fritz, the fashionable artist of the Sebastiansplatz—the moment the lights went out in the Sebastiansplatz, as it were, when there were no more parties and no longer anything to be gained by going there. She pretended to be her closest friend, whereas she had been a deserter from Joana's cause for years. And then she had arranged for her wreath to have this dreadful bow with the words *From Jeannie* attached to it, in the belief that this would somehow cancel out years of disloyalty, I thought. And I thought to myself: she hates me because, contrary to her wishes, I finally became a writer, no matter what kind of a writer—a writer all the same, in other words a competitor, and not an actor or a producer or a theater manager, as she would have liked me to become. This, after all, was the reason why one day she introduced me to Joana, I thought. At all costs she wanted to prevent my becoming a writer, I thought, but now that I had become one she hated me for it. In her eyes I had committed a capital offense by becoming a writer in spite of everything—in spite of everything, I am bound to repeat, in spite of all her efforts to prevent me. And I thought of all the venom with which she had pursued me during the last twenty years in the pages of her journal *Literature in Our Time*, of the way she had put down everything I had published—or tried to put it down. And when she was not trying to put down my writings herself by publishing vicious articles and defamatory essays about them in her *Literature in Our Time*, she did not recoil from exploiting others in pursuit of her vendetta, penniless writers who were forced to rely on her, I now thought. But it was ridiculous to get so worked up: by getting myself worked up over something so non-sensical I was making myself ridiculous in my own eyes, and I told myself several times, though in such a way that only *I* could hear it: *You're making yourself ridiculous, you're making yourself ridiculous in your own eyes—you've made yourself ridiculous in your own eyes. What a disgusting character you are!* The words were addressed only to myself—no one else could hear them—and I went on addressing myself, working myself into a state of growing agitation. *You* betrayed Jeannie—*she* didn't betray *you*, I told myself more than once, and I went on repeating it to myself until I was utterly exhausted. It was already half past two in the morning, and we were still sitting in the dining room. The actor was still talking and the others listening: throughout this *artistic dinner* he was virtually the only person who said anything, because nearly every-one else was much too tired to talk. The only others who made any contribution to the conversation were Jeannie Billroth—who every now and then said something that seemed to me invariably inept or ineffectual, though at times vicious and rude—and the Auersbergers themselves. None of the other guests said a single word—and there were seven or eight of them at this *artistic dinner*, or per-haps ten or twelve. For a long time I was not sure how many guests there were or whether I knew them all. I did know them all, of course, but I paid no attention to most of them—they were simply part of the scenery, I thought. One actually finds most people uninteresting, I thought, all the time—almost all the people we meet are uninteresting, having nothing to offer us but their collective mediocrity and their collective imbecility, with which they bore us on every occasion, and so naturally we have no time for them. If we look back, I thought, we see that they have quite automatically made themselves ludicrous and uninteresting in their thousands, their tens of thousands, their millions. How tiresome and insignificant celebrities like this Burgtheater actor can be! I now thought as I suddenly saw him yawn, after which the hostess yawned, and then Auersberger yawned. At this point they probably all yawned. Jeannie and I were the only two who did not, and by now we were staring fixedly at each other. The Virginia Woolf of Vienna, who remained simply the wife of Ernstl the chemist, was already as old at sixty as some people become only when they reach seventy or eighty, I thought. I recalled *The Wilderness of Youth* and all the nonsense she had put into it, in the belief that it was world-class literature, whereas it was only petit bourgeois kitsch. She hates you, I told myself, and you despise her—that's the truth of it. But she hates you not just because you left her more than twenty years ago—twenty-five years ago in fact—and because you're a writer, but because you're ten years her junior. Such women never forgive you for the fact that they are ten years older than you, I thought. She hates me because I left her to go on living with her Ernstl in their apartment in the Second District and went over to Joana, exchanging the writer who was ten years older than myself for the movement artist who was only six years older, and who had a Fritz instead of an Ernstl. All the same Jeannie still has her Ernstl, whereas for the last eighteen years of her life Joana didn't have her Fritz, I thought. She now hates me with a far greater hatred than twenty-five or twenty years ago, I thought. *She hates you with a fundamental hatred*, I told myself. No no, if the

Auersbergers had said that they were inviting Jeannie to their *artistic dinner*, I wouldn't have come to the Gentzgasse, I thought. I always make the mistake of not asking the hosts who else is being invited, I thought. Had they said, We've invited Jeannie Billroth too, I would never have come to the Gentzgasse. And so at once I fell into the Gentzgasse trap on two counts, on three or four counts, on a thousand counts, it seemed to me. I ought to have known that Jeannie would obviously be coming to an *artistic dinner* like this in the Gentzgasse, especially as it was taking place on the day of Joana's funeral; and it was equally obvious that she would be coming without Ernstl, whom she has never taken to visit her artistic friends, I thought, and who never had any interest in artists or anything to do with artists, who never showed the slightest interest in anything that interested Jeannie, I have to say. Nothing that interested Jeannie was ever of the slightest interest to her Ernstl: he was interested only in chemistry and Jeannie herself, nothing else—only in his chemistry and the conjugal bed. And this was the one day, I thought, when I ought not to have laid myself open to Jeannie's malice, for the effect she had on me was not only destructive, but annihilating; what is more, she at once realized this and gave me no quarter. There was no longer any way of escaping her: I might have got up and left, but I was already too weak to do this; on the other hand I thought I would be able to survive this night in the Gentzgasse, as I had survived hundreds of equally intolerable late-night parties there—after all I've survived all of them up to now, I thought. The actor from the Burgtheater had settled himself in one of the chairs in the music room. He was naturally the first to take his place; only after he had sat down did the others find themselves places in various parts of the room. Once again I was the last, and as I dragged myself into the music room I thought, Ah yes, no doubt Auersberger's wife is now going to sing us one or two arias. Auersberger had the *Purcell Music Book* open in readiness, but as it was now three o'clock I hoped that she would refrain from treating us to a sample of her art. And in fact I was spared having to listen to her singing, though I am bound to say that she always sang with great charm; indeed she had a particularly beautiful voice, I might even say an extremely fine voice, I thought as I took my place in the music room. This too was furnished in the Empire style and full of treasures which no one could afford today, as it had been thirty years ago. Some were heirlooms which Auersberger's father-in-law had brought to Vienna from Styria, from the family residence in Maria Zaal; others he had acquired in Vienna on highly favorable terms, having been well acquainted, as I happen to know, with an antique dealer in the Third District, who for various reasons preferred to call himself a *secondhand dealer*, although essentially he dealt only in valuable items. This so-called secondhand dealer had for years done business, on a *quid pro quo* basis, with Auersberger's father-in-law, who treated him for his various illnesses and was in return supplied with all kinds of Josephine and Empire furniture, as well as some exquisite Biedermeier pieces, without having to pay a penny for them. Thirty years ago, I thought, I used to love this music room, which I always described as the most beautiful Josephine room I had ever seen. But later I realized that it was simply *too* beautiful, *too* perfectly furnished, and hence unbearable. Looking around the room now, I found it merely repugnant, probably because in the intervening years I had ceased to place such a high value on rooms like this which were furnished solely with antiques;

my early enthusiasm for old furniture had diminished and turned almost to dislike. People furnish their apartments in an antique style, surrounding themselves with furniture that is centuries old, furniture from an age that does not concern them, and this makes them guilty of a certain kind of mendacity, I thought. Being too feeble to cope with their own age, one might say, they find it necessary, in order to keep themselves above water, to surround themselves with furniture from a bygone age, an age that is dead and gone, I thought. It really is a sign of appalling feebleness, I thought, if people fill their apartments with furniture belonging to past ages rather than their own, the harshness and brutality of which they are unable to endure. What they do, it seems to me, is surround themselves with the softness of the dead past that cannot answer back. The Auersbergers, who have always been credited with what is called taste, have never had any real taste, but only a secondhand surrogate, just as they have no life, no existence of their own, but only a secondhand surrogate. It was not they who were the focal point of their parties, I thought, but their furniture, their *objets d'art* and their money. They don't speak for themselves: they let their furniture and their money speak for them, just as they've done tonight, I thought. As this thought struck me, their true indigence was borne in upon me. The Auersbergers believe themselves to be objects of admiration, yet the truth is that those who visit them really admire only their furniture, their *objets d'art*, and the skill with which these are disposed about their residences. They think people admire *them*, I thought, while in fact people admire only their polished cabinets and sideboards, their tables and chairs, the many oil paintings on their walls, and their money. It is by no means farfetched to think that what people admire about them, what draws people to them and inspires admiration, is their wealth, and the more or less shameless life-style it enables them to sustain. It's not only the emperor's clothes that make the emperor, but the emperor's furniture and art treasures, I thought. But in the dimly lit music room it's quite impossible to see any of these art treasures, I thought—not that I had any wish to see them, for I would undoubtedly have been sickened by the sight. How sickened I was by this whole apartment in the Gentzgasse, which once more struck me as perversely ostentatious! Such perfection, which hits you in the eye and crowds in upon you from all sides, is simply repellent, I thought, just as all apartments are repellent in which everything is *just so*, as they say, in which nothing is ever out of place or ever permitted to be out of place. We find such apartments repellent and would never feel at home in them, I thought, unless we were to some extent absentminded, as I was thirty years ago when I first set foot in this apartment. Being the last to take my place, I found myself sitting between the actor and Auersberger. The former now looked like a retired infantry general, and I noticed that even his loquacity had been dampened by the large intake of food: he had suddenly become silent, and as he sat with his legs stretched out in front of him there was something military about his whole demeanor, I thought. Such knife-edge creases are seen only in officers' trousers, I thought—generals' trousers, field marshals' trousers. The hostess was circulating among the guests with a decanter of white wine, but by now everybody was tired and showed scarcely any interest in the wine or any other drink. Only Auersberger continued to drink nonstop. He was probably due for another drying-out cure at Kalksburg, I thought, looking at him from the side—at the sunken temples and the fat spongy cheeks that hung from them. Had the sight not been so repulsive I would have thought it merely grotesque, but I was devastated to see him in this condition. This is somebody you were once more or less in love with, I thought to myself as I viewed him from the side; there was a time when it might have been said that you'd fallen in love with this man. And now he was sitting next to me, I thought, puffy and bloated, able to draw attention to himself only by mumbling something from time to time in a drink-sodden voice. He's wearing those grotesque knitted socks again, I thought, and that utterly tasteless peasant jacket, and that linen shirt with the color-ful embroidery and stiff collar, which looks even more ridiculous on him than it would on anyone else. His wife obviously suffered under her husband's perversely de-mented condition, which she could do nothing about. An hour earlier she had tried, without success, to persuade him to leave the party and go to bed; now she made a second attempt to get her husband, who had meanwhile drunk him-self into a thoroughly infantile condition, out of his chair, out of the music room, and into his bed, but Auersberger pushed her away with a full glass of wine in his hand; in doing so he hurt her eye and spilled the wine on the floor, at the same time calling her a *silly goose*, as he had done throughout the evening. He had behaved no differently thirty years earlier. I was used to these scenes at the Auers-bergers'—I know them well. The present one was rela-tively innocuous. Such evenings usually ended with Auersberger flinging his wine glass against the wall and smashing up one of the priceless Empire chairs. Their chairs were constantly having to be repaired by a restorer in the city center who made a good deal of money out of the Auersbergers' mania for destruction. Every now and then Auersberger succeeded in saying something, even in getting whole sentences out. One of these was *The human race ought to be abolished,* a pronouncement with which he more than once attracted the attention of the company in the music room, delivering it with a rhythmic precision that came from his musical training. He delivered himself of other pronouncements, such as: *Society ought to be abolished* and *We should all kill one another.* I was too familiar with such pronouncements to find them original, but on this occasion I was not embarrassed by them, as the others no doubt were, not having heard them before, among them the actor from the Burgtheater, who had clearly not heard them before this evening and found them embarrassing, as I could see. *But my dear Auersberger,* he said, *what's the matter with you? Why are you getting so worked up? The world's a beautiful place and the people in it are good people. Why do you get so worked up and run everything down when everything is essentially so agreeable and well ordered?* Having said this, he added, *Why do you have to drink yourself almost into a stupor?* He shook his head and drew on his cigar, which the hostess had lighted for him. Jeannie Billroth, sitting opposite me, remained silent, observing the scene between Auersberger, with whom she had been even more infatuated than I had been twenty-five years earlier, and the Burgtheater actor, with whom she had hoped to have what she always termed an *intellectual conversation,* though no such conversation had materialized: the actor had not been willing to respond to any of her questions or enter into any discussion with her, and thus had given her no chance to strike up an *intellectual conversation,* choosing rather to confine his attention to the genuine Balaton pike and the recounting of his own anecdotes. Jeannie always wanted to have *intellectual conversations* and took every opportunity to stress that this was all that mattered to her in her social dealings, that this was her sole motive for attending parties; but most of the time she had no precise notion—or even a rough notion—of what constituted an *intellectual conversation*. She doubtless thought that an actor from the Burgtheater would be just the right partner for an *intellectual conversation*, but she was wrong. An *intellectual conversation* was the last thing the actor wanted that evening: he had not even been willing to talk about ordinary topics of supposedly intellectual interest or even to discuss matters that might be thought germane to his profession. Jeannie had repeatedly tried to lure him out of his reserve, as it were; she did not know that he had no reserve—nor could he have, I reflected, since he was after all an actor from the Burgtheater, one of the many half-wits engaged to perform there, who remain within their narrow intellectual confines, their generally mindless confines, and reach a venerable old age on the national stage. Even *this* actor's face betrays no sign of anything that might be called remotely intellectual, I told myself, but Jeannie failed to see this. Even so, there was a certain tactlessness in inviting an actor to talk about the theater or the acting profession, in other words about his livelihood: nobody likes doing this, nobody finds it acceptable or tolerable to have to give his views on what he is obliged to live with, namely his profession—what some might call his vocation. She herself has always refused to talk about writing, and so have I, for naturally, as a writer I hate nothing so much as having to discuss writing. I've always refused to do so, and in this way I've offended a great many people, though their tactlessness has always merited whatever offense I've given, I thought. I find nothing so repugnant as talking about writing, and I find it supremely repugnant to talk about my own.

Yet Jeannie imagined that she could talk to the actor about acting at the Burgtheater, I thought. Sitting next to her was Anna Schreker, a high school teacher whom I have also known as long as I have known the Auersbergers and whom I have always seen in their company, though only in the Gentzgasse, never at Maria Zaal, and always with her male companion, who is also a writer. She still has the same revolting sibilant pronunciation she had thirty years ago, I thought. People have always maintained that Anna Schreker the high school teacher is the Austrian Gertrude Stein or the Austrian Marianne Moore, whereas she has only ever been the Austrian Schreker, a local Viennese writer of megalomaniac pretensions. I now recalled that she too had started writing in the fifties, following more or less the same path as Jeannie Billroth, the path that leads from youthful promise to state patronage —starting off as a derivative literary virgin and ending up as a derivative literary matron—the path of mediocrity, it seems to me, not of genius. Just as Jeannie progressed from her Virginia Woolf fixation to her Virginia Woolf posture, so Schreker progressed from her Marianne Moore and Gertrude Stein fixation to her Marianne Moore and Gertrude Stein posture. At an early stage both Jeannie and Schreker, together with Schreker's companion, made a radical break with their early intentions, their early literary visions and passions, and applied themselves instead to the loathsome art of exploiting literature as a means of ingratiating themselves with the state; all three applied themselves with the same abhorrent zeal to the cultivation of various city councillors, ministers, and other officials concerned with cultural affairs, so that as far as I was concerned they suddenly died overnight in the early sixties of their innate feebleness of character and became precisely the kind of sickening, revolting figures they had always accused others of being and spoken of with such supreme contempt. It seems to me that in endeavoring to ingratiate themselves with the state, Schreker and Jeannie betrayed not only themselves, but literature as a whole. This is what I thought at the time, when I suddenly became aware of their ambitions, and what I still think today; I shall never forgive them for what they did, and I am not sure which of the two is the more contemptible. Suddenly, in the early sixties, both Jeannie Billroth and Anna Schreker, in their appallingly opportunistic fashion, positively *crawled* into the very *filth* they had always found so loathsome and been so loud in condemning in the fifties. In the fifties, when I was twenty, they had described the state to me in terms which still hold good today, namely as an institution that brings unmitigated disaster on our benighted nation, yet in the early sixties they seem to have had no compunction in capitulating to this selfsame state and making common cause with it. As I see it, Schreker and Billroth sold out unreservedly to this egregious state in the early sixties, and so from then on I wanted nothing more to do with them, and especially with Jeannie. Schreker I had always regarded as a peripheral phenomenon, though she and Jeannie always struck me as being moral and spiritual siblings. While Jeannie always had her Virginia Woolf madness and hence suffered from a kind of Viennese Virginia Woolf disease, Schreker always had the Marianne Moore and Gertrude Stein madness and suffered from the Marianne Moore and Gertrude Stein disease. At the beginning of the sixties both of them quite suddenly turned their literary madnesses and their literary diseases, which in the fifties had no doubt been quite *genuine* madnesses and quite *genuine* diseases, into a pose, a purpose-built literary pose, a multipurpose literary pose, in order to make themselves attractive to openhanded politicians, thus unscrupulously killing off whatever literature they had inside them for the sake of a venal existence as recipients of state patronage. For I can only describe this pair as devious beneficiaries of state handouts, who in recent years have never missed an opportunity of showing themselves compliant to the perversely openhanded state they once despised, and who in the last fifteen years have been seen *wherever something was up for grabs*, as they say, never failing to take their places at official state functions or civic festivities. Wherever the politicians who run the nation's cultural affairs with such outrageous insolence turn up with their well-filled money bags, these two may be seen dancing attendance. Thus over recent years Jeannie Billroth and Anna Schreker, the two literary, artistic and cultural ladies of my youth, on whom I had for years been prepared to *bet my bottom dollar*, as they say, have come to earn my detestation—Jeannie naturally more so than Schreker, since I never had such close contacts (or conflicts!) with her as I did with Jeannie. It became clear to me at the beginning of the sixties that these two writers, whom I had looked up to in the fifties as the two great female authors of my youth, were merely a couple of petit bourgeois women intent upon dressing up their mendacious inanities in literary guise. And there they were sitting opposite me, the two female monsters of Austrian literature side by side, each as repellent as the other in her inflated literary pretensions. There sit the Marianne Moore, the Gertrude Stein and the Virginia Woolf of Vienna, I thought, and yet they are nothing but devious, ambitious little state *protégées*, who have betrayed literature—and art in general—for the sake of a few ludicrous prizes and a guaranteed pension, kowtowing to the state and its cultural riffraff, churning out their derivative kitsch for the vilest of motives and spending their time going up and down the stairs of the ministries that dole out subventions. How Schreker used to inveigh—indeed vituperate—against the so-called *Art Senate!* Yet a year ago she let this same *Art Senate* single her out for the award of the *Great Austrian State Prize for Literature.* It's nauseating, I thought, to have to watch Schreker and Billroth suddenly falling upon the neck of the former President of the so-called *Art Senate,* now its Honorary President, the very person they execrated for decades and pronounced so dreadful and dangerous, simply because they covet the *Great Austrian State Prize*—to see them suddenly and quite unashamedly fawning upon this man and his acolytes, who have this prize—and the money that goes with it—in their gift. For decades these two women regarded this President of the Art Senate as an object of opprobrium, but now Schreker embraces him in the so-called audience chamber of the Ministry of Culture, check in hand, and makes a fulsome speech of thanks. This Honorary President and former President of the Austrian Art Senate is now ninety years old, yet the decision as to who should be awarded the highest distinction the country has to offer and who should not still rests solely with this stupid, vulgar, arch-Catholic exploiter of the arts, who for decades, it seems to me, has been the greatest polluter of the country's cultural environment, yet Schreker, with the prize at last in her hands, now even kisses him on the cheek—the thought of it still nauseates me. And it will not be long before Billroth and then Schreker's companion march into the audience chamber at the Ministry of Culture to receive the *Great Austrian State Prize* from the hands of this revolting man, and nothing will stop them kissing his cheek and delivering a fulsome speech of thanks. But Billroth and Schreker (and her companion) are not the only people who make a point of cultivating the people who administer state moneys and state honors in this country: almost all Austrian artists go the same way when once they have *reached years of discretion*, as they say, recanting everything they professed and propagated with the utmost vehemence before the age of twenty-five or thirty as the minimal morality required of the artist, in order to ally themselves with those who dispense state moneys, state orders, and state pensions. All Austrian artists end up letting themselves be bought out by the state for its nefarious purposes, selling themselves to this vile, unprincipled, execrable state, and most of them start off that way. Their art consists solely in working hand in glove with the state—that is the truth. Schreker and her companion and Jeannie Billroth are just three examples of the so-called artistic world of Austria. To be an artist in Austria means for most people being compliant to the state, whatever its political complexion, and letting oneself be supported by it for the term of one's natural life. Artistic life in Austria is a road built by state opportunism out of people's baseness and mendacity, paved with scholarships and prizes, lined with decorations and distinctions, and leading to an honored grave in the Central Cemetery. Schreker, who is incapable of developing a simple idea and has for decades written nothing but drivel, passes for an intellectual writer in the same way as Billroth, who in my opinion is even stupider, I thought. This fact is characteristic not only of the *degenerate intellectual life of Austria*, but of intellectual life generally. But in Austria this catastrophic state of affairs seems even more catastrophic if, having just come from England, we observe it from a bird's-eye view. The repellent has always been more repellent here, the tasteless always more tasteless, the ludicrous always more ludicrous. But what and where would we be, I wonder, if things were different? Schreker, her companion, and Jeannie, who for twenty years have been simulating rebelliousness, revolution, and advanced attitudes for the benefit of the young, while in reality expending all their energy running up and down the back stairs of the ministries that hand out the money, have always been intellectual birds of a feather; I have always been repelled by the skill they display in hoodwinking the young and blackmailing the benighted ministries. Anna Schreker is now sitting next to Jeannie Billroth, I thought, and I observed the two of them, these degenerate *spiritual siblings*. Schreker and Billroth and Schreker's companion are today the embodiment of the kind of derivative pseudo-intellectual literary garbage that I've always detested, though it's lapped up by fashion-crazed whiz-kid copy readers who've never outgrown their literary puberty, and eagerly subsidized by senile officials of the Ministry of Culture in the Minoritenplatz. This evening, for this *artistic dinner*, I thought, Schreker has come dressed all in black, as always. Now she was suddenly sitting in the background next to the one-armed painter Rehmden, a member of the so-called *Second Viennese Surrealist School* and naturally a professor at the art academy in the Schillerplatz, *the nature engraver with the fine line*. Auersberger, whom I once in all seriousness called a *Novalis of sound*, as I now recall to my horror, had long since become *unaccountable for his actions* and did no more than mumble the occasional incomprehensible remark. Earlier, no doubt in a final effort to attract everyone's attention, he had suddenly removed his lower dental plate and held it in front of the actor's face, remarking that life was short, man a frail creature, and death not far away. This had prompted the actor to utter the word *tasteless* several times, while Auersberger replaced the dental plate in his mouth. His wife naturally jumped up once more, intending to get him out of the music room and into the bedroom. Again she did not succeed; Auersberger threatened several times to kill her and pushed her away, so that she stumbled against the actor, who caught her in his arms, whereupon Auersberger exclaimed *Oh how tasteless!* several times, then dozed off in his peasant jacket. Also present at this *artistic dinner* were two young men who spoke with a Styrian dialect; these hefty country louts were probably related to Auersberger, I thought, and had been dragged along, in the true sense of the phrase, to *beef up the artistic dinner*, as they say. For as long as I observed them they spoke to nobody but each other, just as I conversed with nobody but myself; having come to this *artistic dinner*, I remained more or less silent throughout the whole proceedings, it now occurs to me. In other words I behaved in much the same way as the two young men, who were said to be trainee engineers, except that they for some reason kept on standing up and sitting down again, whereas I remained seated nearly all the time, first in the anteroom and then at the dining table. Only on two occasions did I speak to anyone. On the first occasion it was to ask the actor whether, after four or five decades, he was not sick to the teeth, as they say, of constantly playing classical roles at the Burgtheater —Goethe *or* Shakespeare and Grillparzer, *Goethe or Shakespeare twice a year* and *Grillparzer once every two or three years*, but a role like Ekdal in *The Wild Duck* only every five or six years, or alternatively playing in some silly English society comedy like the one the Burgtheater was now rehearsing, but he did not answer me. The other occasion was when I told Auersberger, quite superfluously, that he had made a mess of his life and dragged his genius in the dirt for the sake of a rich wife and high living, that he had destroyed himself in the process and made drinking the be-all and end-all of his life, that he had exchanged one misfortune, that of his youth, for a second misfortune, that of old age, that he had sacrificed his musical genius for his revolting socializing, and intellectual freedom for the bondage of wealth. I also told him several times that I found his peasant-style woolen jacket distasteful, and his peasant-style linen shirt equally so—that in fact I found everything about him distasteful. I attended this *artistic dinner* but, like the two Styrian louts, I took no part in it; I observed the proceedings without involving myself in them. There were one or two other people in the background whom I had been unable to identify even in the dining room, which was much more brightly lit than the music room, and then there were the two young writers, who made their presence felt by repeatedly bursting into peals of laughter, though the reason for their laughter escaped me. It had begun to get on my nerves even before the Burgtheater actor arrived on the scene: it was a completely hollow and mindless laughter, such as we often hear nowadays when we are with young people—hollow, inane and mindless. The two young writers had virtually nothing to say for themselves, I thought; they drank incessantly and ate everything that was set before them, and although they had been invited to this *artistic dinner*, probably by Auersberger, to represent *artistic intellectual youth at the dinner table*—as a counterpoise to the two technological youths from Styria—they took no active part in it. But what, after all, can young writers have to say? I thought. They imagine they know everything, yet can only find everything ridiculous, without being able to say *why* it's ridiculous. This is something they don't discover until much later, I thought. At first they find everything ridiculous, without knowing why, then later they know why, but don't tell anybody, because they've no reason to do so. This is the stupid, hollow, mindless laughter that's typical of today's youth, the youth of our own age, the perverse, mindless, dangerous eighties, I thought. They burst into peals of laughter and find everything ridiculous and haven't published a single book, I thought—just like you thirty years ago. They've got nothing but their laughter, nothing, and they're content with it. All they have is their laughter: the catastrophe of life still lies ahead of them, I thought. They have only their laughter, and no way of justifying it. And I recalled how I, as just such a young writer, had sat at parties like this and spent all my time laughing, finding everything laughable, but never giving a reason, and taking no part in the proceedings apart from drinking and eating and laughing. I found the two young men so uninteresting—just as uninteresting as I had been—that I made no approach to them, just as no one had made any approach to me when I was their age, I told myself. We don't learn anything of interest by talking to the youth of the eighties: we talk and talk and talk, without understanding what we're talking about, and they talk and talk and talk, and we don't understand a word of what they say, nor do we want to understand, I told myself. Talking to young people gets us nowhere, I thought, and anyone who asserts the contrary is a hypocrite, for young people have nothing to say to their elders, to old people—that's the truth. What the young have to say to the old is of absolutely no interest, none whatever, I thought, and to assert the contrary is gross hypocrisy. It's always been fashionable to say that the old should talk to the young because they've so much to learn from them, but the opposite is the truth: the young have nothing whatever to say to the old. Of course the old would have something to say to the young, but the young don't understand what the old have to say to them, and, being unable to understand, they've no wish to understand. Auersberger always had young writers in his entourage and in his bed, I now recalled; I was one of the first to be invited to Maria Zaal—one of the first to walk into his trap, one of the first to play the fool for him. *Someone to paper over the marital cracks*, I said to myself, *the marital cracks on both walls*, I added, looking at the two young writers and the two trainee engineers. Auersberger was not content to take just any young men to bed with him, I thought—they had to be *young writers*. He never invited a young painter or a young sculptor to go to Maria Zaal and share his bed: only a young writer would do. He would invite him to go to Maria Zaal and then invite him to share his bed, intending to devour him, I now thought. He would pay his fare to Maria Zaal, no matter where from, pick him up from the station, and show him to the room that had been prepared for him, and on the very first day he would try to devour him. This thought had sickened and tormented me for years, indeed for decades, but all at once it no longer did. *Auersberger, the lecherous literary Moloch*, I thought, and had I not been so tired I could have laughed out loud at this formulation of mine. *Auersberger and the young writers*, I thought —I could write a short essay on the subject, or even a long essay—*an essay and a half*, as they say. I'll certainly play Ekdal another fifty times or so, the actor said suddenly. He was now leaning back in his chair with his eyes closed. If only I'd had someone better to play Gregers! I ought

to have played Gregers myself, but that's an absurd idea—
playing both Ekdal and Gregers simultaneously! That's
absurd! Quite absurd! said the actor. Meanwhile Auersberger's wife had put on a record of Ravel's *Bolero*, which
had been Joana's favorite piece. She's chosen the *Bolero*
on purpose to remind us of Joana, I said to myself. And
no sooner had I heard the opening bars than I began to
think of Joana again, and above all of her funeral. At first
I thought it tasteless to play a record of the *Bolero*, but
perhaps it was not. Possibly it was a good idea, however
contrived, to turn this more or less frightful supper, this
artistic dinner, into an act of remembrance for Joana. Before she put the record on I had already made up my mind
to get up and leave, but now I was quite happy to go on
sitting there, suddenly feeling pleasantly indifferent to everything, letting the images of the funeral float through my
mind. I had a clear vision of the scenes in the *Iron Hand*,
the face of the woman from the general store, and John's
face, and Kilb, the beautiful, restful little market town in
Lower Austria. The *agitation* I had felt throughout this
dreadful evening and night in the Gentzgasse suddenly
gave way to a sense of *calm*. I have always enjoyed listening to the *Bolero*, which Joana always played in her movement studio when she was working with her more gifted
pupils. Actually the whole of her art of movement and
the whole of her teaching was oriented to the *Bolero*, I
thought, as I listened to the music with my eyes closed.
How good it feels to be sentimental now and then, I
thought. I could now see Joana quite clearly, the movement artist who had had every chance of happiness but
whose life had ended in utter misery. I could hear her
voice and take delight in the things she used to say, in her
laugh, in her *responsiveness to everything beautiful*. For

Joana had the gift of always seeing the beauty which exists beside the terrible, unending ugliness that destroys and annihilates—a gift which very few possess, but which she possessed to a higher degree than anyone I have known in my whole life. But even this gift did her no good, I thought. She came to Vienna and let Vienna devour her; then she fled from Vienna and went back home, only to hang herself, I thought. And I recalled how Joana's neighbor, who always looked after the house for her when she was away, had found her just before six o'clock in the morning, hanging from a rope that she had tied in a noose and attached to a roof beam with her own hands. The woman from the general store had broken down in the *Iron Hand*. She told me that the neighbor had at first seen only Joana's feet swinging above the stairs in the entrance hall; going closer she had seen the legs, and finally the whole heavy body, completely bloated from years of drinking, hanging in the noose and set in motion by the opening of the door. It had been a *grotesque* sight, and at the same time *horrible*, said the woman from the general store. The neighbor had not screamed, she said, but stayed *quite calm* and come straight over to her to tell her of her discovery, knowing her to be Joana's best friend. It was not yet light at the time. At seven o'clock Joana's friend had called me in Vienna; I was not the first person she called, but she informed me only an hour after the body was discovered. The *Bolero* gradually brought back all the different stations in Joana's life. I saw her alternately in the Sebastiansplatz, in Kilb, and in Maria Zaal, where she had often been a guest. She loved wearing clothes of her own design, I thought, and ancient Egyptian bracelets and Persian earrings; she had a very keen and very feminine interest in ancient African and Asiatic cultures, about which she read every book and article she could find. She would wrap herself in Indian silks and wear Afghan, Chinese and Turkish necklaces. No one else talked more about her dreams, which she tried to *explore* and trace back to their origins. I used to spend whole nights with her exploring her dreams. She was interested in other people's dreams too; she made a study of them, one might say, and hence the exploration of dreams became her second art, I thought. She often described herself as a *dreamwalker*, leading a *dreamwalking* existence. I remembered how she liked to surround herself with young people—*preferably very young people who can still dreamwalk*, she would say, *who've not yet been spoiled and corrupted by culture and education*. Naturally she had a fantastic feeling for fairy stories, which were her favorite reading, and she liked reading them aloud, sometimes publicly. Dreams and fairy stories were the real stuff of her life, I thought. That was why she killed herself, because a person whose life is built on dreams and fairy stories can't survive in this world—has no right to survive, I thought. She was a fairy-tale figure herself, and no doubt all her life she believed herself to be a figure in a fairy story—Elfriede Slukal, who in the fairy story was called *Joana*, I thought. I must say the *Bolero* was always her piece, the center of her existence. We shouldn't be afraid of letting sentimentality take over from time to time, I thought, and I now let the *Bolero* take over; I let myself go, surrendering myself to the music and my feelings for Joana, until the moment when Jeannie Billroth asked the actor, who was sitting next to me but opposite Jeannie, what he thought of the fact that *a new director was about to enter the house on the Ring*, that the Burgtheater was going to be exposed to a new wind—a fresh wind, some thought, that would sweep out everything in the Burgtheater that was stale and

dead and horrible, everything that had become revolting
and disgusting and appalling over the years. What did he
think of the fact that *one of the best theater people* was
about to move into the Burgtheater, *a German genius, a
German theatrical genius of the first rank, the very first
rank, a first-class theater fanatic*, as Jeannie put it, or rather
as it had been put by others, for she was only quoting what
she had heard or read in the newspapers, she said—she was
not expressing her own opinion about the new man from
Germany, whom she did not know, who still had to con-
vince her, who was still an unknown quantity as far as she
was concerned. *A theatrical tornado*, the papers had said,
*an elemental man of the theater such as the Burgtheater had
not seen for a hundred years* was about to move into the
Burgtheater, if she might venture to quote what the papers
had said. The Burgtheater actor, who had dozed off briefly,
was startled by this sudden question. *So, what do you think
of this new man who's coming to your theater?* Jeannie
persisted, as though she had at last found a quarry for the
malice that had been lying in wait all evening and suddenly
saw how to bring her quarry to bay and dispatch it. *But
surely you have an opinion about the new man?* she said
several times. At this the actor became indignant; he sat
up in his chair, drew in his legs, raised his head high, and
said, Good, fine, so a new man's taking over. But that was
of no interest to him, he said, it could no longer be of any
interest to him. He had seen so many directors take up the
post only to lose it again that this new man was of no interest to him. They come and they go, he said, they're
received with open arms and then ignominiously sent pack-
ing. It had always been like that, he said, and the new man
would be no exception. All right, he said, the new man may
be a genius, as you say. To this Jeannie replied that *she*

had not said he was a genius—that was what the newspapers had said. It was not she who had said it, but the
papers. Every day one read something in the papers about
this genius from Germany, she went on—it was not *she*
who had said it. The Burgtheater actor replied, Whether
the papers say it or whether you say it, my dear, it's a
matter of complete indifference to me who the new man
is who's taking over. It had always been a matter of indifference to him, he said. He had *outlived ten or eleven
Burgtheater directors who had all vanished without trace*—
nobody could remember their names any longer. They're
appointed by the minister, who has no idea about the theater
and is guided only by his political instinct. *They work for
a year and then they're shed*, said the actor, suddenly becoming heated again. The minister appoints the man he
thinks will be most useful to him, naturally *always for
political reasons, never for artistic reasons*, and no sooner
has the new man signed the contract than he encounters
hostility, and every effort is made to get him out as quickly
as possible. Two or three productions get good notices, and
then the critics start attacking and destroying the man
they've just praised for a whole year before he signed the
contract. If the newspapers say he's a genius *before* he's
signed the contract and taken up his post, they'll call him
an idiot *afterwards*. No matter what productions he puts
on, they'll attract less and less praise, and in two or three
years he'll be no good at all, said the actor. If he stages
classical plays it'll be stupid, and if he stages modern plays
it'll be equally stupid. If he favors Austrian playwrights
it'll be wrong, and if he goes for foreign playwrights it'll
be equally wrong. If, before coming to the Burgtheater,
he's been told that his Shakespeare productions are *over-
whelming, altogether the best Shakespeare productions* the

critics have ever seen, he'll be told they're a disaster as soon as he's in his post at the Burgtheater. The kingmakers of the Burgtheater turn into regicides the moment they've achieved their aim and the new king is on the throne, he said. Ah, you know, he said to Jeannie Billroth, if you're a good actor you don't care who the theater director is. A new director loses his attraction in no time. Hardly has he been seen in the Kärntnerstrasse a few times or dined once or twice at the Sacher or the Imperial, than he's finished. There have always been favorite actors at the Burgtheater, my dear, but there's never been a favorite director. If you really want to know, it's a matter of complete indifference to me who's going to succeed our present director, he said. Suddenly everyone was listening with the greatest interest, and the actor was now not only smoking a cigar, but drinking white wine. The actors at the Burgtheater put down roots in Vienna, he said. They buy properties in Grinzing and Hietzing and Sievering and Neustift, and they live out their boring lives in their boring villas until they reach their boring old age, but the directors of the Burgtheater haven't the slightest chance of putting down roots in this beautiful city. Woe betide any director who buys himself a house here: before he's even moved into it he'll be frozen out or kicked out. The story of the directors of the Burgtheater is not just a scandalous story, said the actor, it's possibly the saddest of all Viennese stories. Vienna is an *art mill*, the biggest art mill in the world, in which the arts and artists are ground down and pulverized year in, year out; whatever the art or whatever the artists, the Viennese art mill grinds them all to powder. It grinds *everything* to powder—*everything*, said the actor, *quite ineluctably*. And the curious thing is that all these people jump into this art mill entirely of their own volition, only to be totally ground down by it. Even the Burgtheater directors jump into it of their own free will, having in some cases spent their whole lives frantically seeking an opportunity to do so, falling over themselves to jump into this art mill in which they'll be totally ground down. *Totally ground down, totally pulverized*, exclaimed the actor. But the sensations and scandals surrounding an outgoing or an incoming director of the Burgtheater have never affected me. You see, my dear, he said, still addressing Jeannie Billroth, I'd have played Ekdal under any director, believe me. And in any case, he said, as though wishing to close the subject, I'll have retired before the new director takes office. I shan't be around when he takes over. He now turned to Auersberger, who had been dozing all the time and heard nothing of the actor's reply to Jeannie Billroth's question. You know, he said, when I've retired I'll be quite content to give two or three readings a year at the Konzerthaus, from the works of Rilke or the late Goethe. I'm not really interested in the theater of today. If I had my way I'd be retired already, because nowadays everything to do with the theater is intolerable. Once upon a time it was a pleasure to be an actor—it was one's mission in life—but I no longer get anything out of it. Nobody is more surprised than myself that I'm playing Ekdal and having such a success in the role, he said. But the truth is, the theater no longer has my interest. You see, he said, turning to Jeannie, I've had so many happy years on the stage, and I don't regret a single day I've spent in the theater—I don't regret a single hour of the happy time I've spent at the Burgtheater. But I no longer get anything out of it, said the actor. To this Jeannie replied that in her opinion the reason why he had got nothing out of the theater for so long was that he had been unable to tear himself away from the Burgtheater. *You've got nothing out of the theater for such a long time*, she said, *because you've bought a property in Grinzing—because you've dined at the Sacher every day and gone to the Café Mozart for coffee every day.* If you'd left the Burgtheater, or, better still, if you'd left Vienna altogether, you wouldn't now be saying that you'd got nothing out of the theater for such a long time. Possibly it was because you bought a property in Grinzing that you lost your enjoyment of the theater and theatrical affairs generally, Jeannie insisted. Possibly you're right, my dear, the actor replied, but I suspect you're probably not. There's been a general decline in the theater. No matter whether you're in Vienna or elsewhere, you no longer find good theater. The theater has lost its fascination. I don't believe that, said Auersberger, whom everyone had long assumed to be asleep. He gave it as his opinion that the theater was as alive as it had ever been. It was only in Vienna that it had gone stale—not just moribund, but *actually dead, actually dead, actually dead*, he exclaimed, after which he repeated these words several times, but now in a drunken mumble. Because his mumbling sounded so comic the two young writers began to laugh. Having been to all intents and purposes absent throughout the evening, they now laughed out loud at Auersberger's intervention. *My God!* the actor exclaimed suddenly. *A theatrical genius —what's that supposed to mean? A director and a genius? What an absurdity!* You know, he said to Jeannie Billroth, the newspapers use the most monstrous language, and everything they print is monstrous. Whatever paper you pick up, you're confronted with something monstrous. Of course we may choose to say that we don't mind what the newspapers print, but all the same we can't help being mortally wounded by it. But the worst papers in the world are the

Austrian papers, in which viciousness reaches its apogee, he said. There are no other papers in which you find such viciousness. Austrian history, indeed world history, has always suffered from the awfulness of these papers, said the actor. Although I've always been praised by them, I still think they're the most awful papers in the world, with the most monstrous and stupid contents. Yet we never fail to read them every day, greedily gulping down everything they print, he said—that's the truth. Ever since I was a child I've been gulping down this Austrian journalistic filth, but I'm still alive. The Austrian stomach is pretty strong. The Austrians in general have strong stomachs, considering what an awful tasteless history they've had to gulp down over the years. Austrian newspapers, if one can call them newspapers, are the world's worst, said the actor, but for precisely that reason they're probably the world's best. Auersberger now responded by mumbling, *You're right there, you're right there. How right you are!* And the two young writers again laughed uproariously. We live in the midst of perpetual absurdity, the actor said suddenly, unadulterated absurdity. I beg you to consider the fact that *everything* is absurd. Absurd ideas are the only true ideas, said the actor. Consider the fact that this absurd world we live in is the only true world. Everything that exists is absurd, said the actor with sudden pathos, and leaned back in his chair. Absurd and perverse, he added. Thereupon he immediately turned to Auersberger's wife and said, *I was so looking forward to hearing a sample of your art.* But never mind—perhaps next time. What were you going to sing for us? Purcell, she replied. Ah, Purcell, said the actor. Purcell is all the rage. Like older music generally. People listen to older music all the time, am I not right? Whereupon Auersberger mumbled, *You're right, you're right, you're right.* Purcell wrote superb songs and arias, said the actor, and looking straight at me he said, It's a rare delight to hear one of them beautifully sung. The *Bolero*—good heavens! he said suddenly, do you know, it always used to get on my nerves? And now I love it. It's the kind of music that gets on our nerves for years, then all at once we love it. You've observed that too, haven't you? he asked Jeannie. Without answering the actor's question, she said, quite unconnectedly, that a new era was about to dawn at the Burgtheater—she actually used the word *dawn*—a new era that would *wipe out* the old. It'll *wipe it out*, she said malevolently. New names will appear and quite different plays will be staged. Yes, that's a good thing, Auersberger mumbled, new names appearing and new plays being staged. *Good-bye to the old favorites*, he mumbled, *good-bye to the remaindered goods, the remaindered goods*. He uttered this last phrase three times, presumably because he liked the sound of it. His wife was probably embarrassed by this remark made by her drunken husband, whose head had by now slumped down into his peasant jacket, for she made yet another fruitless attempt to lift him out of his chair. Auersberger still had enough strength to remind her, by means of a kick in the calf, who was the master in this household in the Gentzgasse. I've just read a book about Palladio, said the actor suddenly, and rediscovered my admiration for the Brenta villas. Forgotten for centuries, he said, then suddenly in vogue again, at the center of world interest, so to speak. I'll go to Spain when I've retired, he said. Not just a short trip as in recent years, but a prolonged stay, months on end. When one's served the theater as long as I have, he said. Actor, mimic, servant of the drama. My greatest good fortune is never to have married; the best thing for an actor is never to embark upon marriage—best to remain alone with one's art, with one's acting. I've always known how to get my way, he said, and curiously enough I've never been ill, not once, apart from minor indispositions, and so I've never had to cancel an appearance, not a single one, whereas my colleagues were forever canceling appearances and in due course developed a kind of cancellation hysteria. *I was never what they call a temperamental actor*, he said, *pedantic perhaps*, but never temperamental, and I never went in for artistic indispositions. An eagerness for knowledge—perhaps that's what it was. Studied every role scientifically, though of course I was the only one who felt the need to do so. I'm not a man for luxury—no, quite the opposite. But not a simple man either—I've always detested simplicity. But in all truth, he went on, here in Vienna the greatest demands are made of the arts, especially of music and acting, greater demands than anywhere else in the whole of Europe. The people who go to the concert halls and the theaters here, and above all the Burgtheater, are utterly spoiled, more exacting and more critical than any other audiences in Europe, I might even say in the whole world. There are no better musicians and actors than the ones you find in Vienna—that's the truth. Go wherever you like, he said, to La Scala in Milan or the Metropolitan in New York, or the National Theatre in London or the Comédie Française —they're all nothing compared with Vienna: ultimately they're all dilettante and amateurish—that's the truth. The Viennese public is the most spoiled in the world, but it's also the most tasteful with regard to both music and theater, while at the same time it's the most infamous and the most ruthless. What ludicrous offerings the German stage presents us with! How inane the English or the French theater is by comparison! But woe betide you if you say this in Vienna, even though it's true. If you dare to say such a thing, you're finished. The acting at the Burgtheater may be as poor as you like, but it's still much better than anything you see on any German stage. No no, said the actor from the Burgtheater, German theater is dilettante and insipid, the kind of brainless theater that has always gone down well with the Germans. German theater has always been amateurish and inept—that's the truth of the matter. Simply modish and mindless—that's the truth. No wit. No imagination. No trace of genius. The actors we see on the German stage perform like schoolteachers, like junior high school teachers. Even the humblest Viennese cabaret artist is superior to the most distinguished German actor, and that's the truth. But tell this truth in Vienna and you'll be stoned. Any Monday night performance at the Burgtheater or the Opera is superior to anything you'll find in the rest of the world. But don't say this in Vienna. It's gratifying to play the part of Ekdal and to have so much success in the part, he went on—to bow out on a note of success. For I don't regard the English role I'm working on as part of my development as an actor: it's something peripheral, not to be taken seriously—not like playing Lear, he said. Just a long-drawn-out paradox, he added. In a way age and indifference go together, he said. In any case I wouldn't want to be young again: it's terrible to be young, but it's not terrible to be old. In fact I wouldn't want to relive a single day of my life, and I'm glad it's not possible. Believe me, said the actor, turning first to the hostess and then to Jeannie, when you're old you become enamored of retirement. People talk about absolutely everything, laugh about absolutely everything, and get themselves worked up about absolutely everything, but none of this affects me any longer. In a certain way, after a life filled with so much art on the stage and so on, one's greatest enjoyment prob-

ably comes from learning the art of being old. The *Bolero*
having come to an end, the hostess got up and went through
the dining room to the kitchen to fetch coffee. Jeannie,
taking advantage of her absence to grab the limelight once
more, asked the actor, who had been gazing at the floor
for some time, *lost in thought* and suddenly completely
exhausted, whether he could say, now that he had more or
less *reached the end of his life*, that he had so to speak *found
fulfillment* in his art. These were the very words with which
she confronted this old man, whom I had found anything
but likable during the course of the evening and night, but
who was by now very tired and deserved to be treated
with some consideration after having played the role of
Ekdal at the Burgtheater only a few hours earlier. *Do
you think that at the end of your life you've found fulfillment in your art?* she asked a second time, as though
he might not have heard her the first time, although he unquestionably had: naturally neither her question nor her
insolence and inconsiderateness had escaped him. She asked
him a third time, *Can you say that at the end of your life
you're fulfilled by your art?* Her insolence did not escape
him this time either, as I saw at once, but he clearly thought
that Jeannie would eventually leave him in peace, since he
had only the most superficial acquaintance with her and she
ought never to have presumed to speak to him in this impudent manner. He was mistaken: Jeannie gave him no
quarter, but put her question several times more. Could he
say, *at the end of his life*, that *his art had brought him fulfillment?* She persisted in her shameless fashion, relentlessly
repeating her question, until the actor was finally forced to
reply, and it was strange to see this man, whom I had
hitherto found thoroughly objectionable and regarded with
the greatest distaste, suddenly give her the answer she de-

served. It was outrageous, he said, to ask him *such a stupid question. Your question is quite simply stupid*, he said. She could surely not expect an intelligent answer to such a stupid and *insolent* question. *I think you've struck the wrong note*, he said, making to get up from his chair, as though he wanted to leave the Auersbergers' Gentzgasse apartment at once and without further ado, having had enough of this insolent questioning. However, seeing the hostess return with the coffee, he sat down again in his armchair, saying as he did so that he did not have to answer stupid questions like that. *Such a tasteless question*, he told the astonished Jeannie, would naturally get no answer from him. *What impertinent nonsense about my coming to the end of my life!* said the actor from the Burgtheater. *What impudent presumption! How rude to confront me with your stupidity!* Jeannie accepted a cup of coffee from Auersberger's wife and suddenly fell silent. She was not in the least indignant, as I had expected her to be. On similar occasions, when her crass stupidity has been shown up, she's always leaped up and left the scene, I recalled. But this time, though bright red in the face under her heavy makeup, she sat motionless for several minutes, while the actor from the Burgtheater, having suddenly recovered his strength, launched into a speech which I found quite astonishing and would never have expected to hear from him. It was distasteful, he said, to mix with people who simply interrogated you and then proceeded to put you down, who were there only to take you apart, as he put it, *to dissect you into all your component parts*; and what was more, to do so after midnight was an additional piece of rudeness. He uttered the word *rudeness* without any apparent compunction, and to my great surprise his hand was not trembling as he held his coffee cup and took an occa-

sional sip from it. We enter a house, thinking it's a friendly
house, he said. Because the actor had recently been so in-
censed, even Auersberger was now wide awake, listening
to what he said. Anna Schreker, the two young writers, and
all the other guests were now listening attentively, for the
actor had again forced everybody's attention on himself
by the strong language he used. Words like *vicious, rude,
insolent, hypocritical, infamous, megalomaniac, stupid* rained
down on the company in the Gentzgasse, and in particular
on Jeannie. He kept on repeating that it was not just ill-
mannered, but positively vicious to confront him with such
stupid questions, as *this person* had done. *This person,* he
said, referring to Jeannie, *was all I needed, this person whom
I instantly loathed, because she's absolutely stupid.* If I'd
known that this person was going to be present, I'd never
have taken up your invitation, the actor told the Auersbergers with some feeling. I hate people like this who are
out to destroy everything, who talk incessantly about art
and have no notion of art, people who blabber away on
evenings like this with a mindlessness that reeks to high
heaven, said the actor indignantly. *When I saw this person
sitting here I thought of turning around and leaving, but
decency forbade me.* He repeated the word *decency* several
times, then leaned back—in relief, I thought, but I was
mistaken. He immediately sat up again, and in a sudden
access of breathlessness he said to Jeannie, You're one of
those people who know nothing and are worth nothing
and consequently hate everybody. It's as simple as that. You
hate everybody because you hate yourself and your own
pitiful inadequacy. You talk incessantly about art, without
having the faintest notion of what art is. He wanted to shout
these words at Jeannie, but he was prevented by his sudden
breathlessness and had to speak them in a monotone. *You're*

a stupid and destructive person, and you're not even ashamed of it, he said, and then fell silent. I have to own that the actor's attack on Jeannie gave me great delight, for I had seldom seen anybody say such things to her face or requite her with such asperity for one of her impertinences. Although I still found the Burgtheater actor repugnant, he had momentarily earned my esteem. Never before has Jeannie Billroth been told how lacking in decency she really is, I thought. Nobody's ever told her that for a long time she's been utterly incompetent in discussing ideas, I thought. Nobody's ever told Jeannie to her face that she's rude, even vulgar, as the actor just has. We feel a great delight when we believe that somebody is getting his just deserts, so to speak, by being reproached with his own rudeness and shamelessness, his own stupidity and incompetence, I thought, especially when we've waited years to see it happen. Jeannie's never before been told that she's basically a common little woman and a low character, but the actor from the Burgtheater has just spelled it out. I had the impression that everyone who witnessed the actor's outburst felt not only a certain momentary pleasure, but a satisfaction that would last rather longer than that. Naturally they did not *express* what they felt: they had no occasion to do so, nor could they have afforded to. The actor could afford to, however, just as I could afford, if only by my silence, to endorse everything he had said about Jeannie. For years, perhaps for decades, we may have wanted to tell someone the truth to his face, the truth that he has never heard because no one has dared to tell it to him to his face, and then at last someone does it for us. And I reflected that by telling Jeannie the truth to her face, whatever that truth may or may not have been, the actor had made it worthwhile for me to have accepted the invitation to the *artistic dinner* after all. *You're a thoroughly dishonest person,* the actor had told her. *For hours you lie in wait for an opportunity to degrade someone. People like you are dangerous. One is well advised to give people like you a wide berth.* Were the actor's words not still ringing in my ears I would not now believe them possible, but they are recorded here exactly as he uttered them that evening. It's quite likely, I thought, that Jeannie had launched her insolent attack on the actor before I left the dining room and entered the music room, that she had for some time been playing the part of the repulsive Jeannie Billroth I know all too well from the time when I was still having an affair with her. She has not changed. If she is not the focus of attention at any gathering, she makes every effort to put this right by mounting what one might call a frontal attack and insulting the person who is meant to be the focus of attention, as the actor from the Burgtheater was at this *artistic dinner.* And she must have started provoking him even before I entered the dining room, for otherwise his angry explosion would have been inexplicable. I now knew the reason for the curious outbursts which I had heard from the music room while I was still sitting in the anteroom and which I did not understand at the time, loud exclamations such as *Ekdal? Rubbish!* or *Gregers? Rubbish!* or *The Wild Duck? Rubbish!* They had clearly been directed at Jeannie when she began her attack. Yes, said the actor, getting up to leave and handing his empty coffee cup to Auersberger's wife, who had also risen from her chair, *how I hate gatherings like this, which seek to destroy everything that means anything to me, to drag everything I've always held dear in the dirt, where people exploit my name and the fact that I'm an actor at the Burgtheater! How I long, not so much for peace, as to be left in peace! If only I'd been born a different person, I've always thought, if only I'd become a completely different person from the one I have become, a person who was left in peace! But then I'd have had to be born of different parents and have grown up in quite different circumstances, surrounded by nature, a nature that was free and unconfined, instead of being surrounded by artificiality. For we've all grown up amid artificiality—not only I, who have always suffered under it, but everyone here.* And turning to Jeannie he added, *Even you, my dear, who pursue me with your hatred and contempt.* He now turned to me, but did not address me. Finally he turned to Auersberger, who was once more asleep in his chair, completely drunk, and remarked that it was a misfortune to have been born at all, but the greatest misfortune of all was *to have been born a person like Herr Auersberg.* To enter into nature, to breathe natural air, to be utterly at home in nature—that, he felt, must be the greatest happiness. *To go into the forest, deep into the forest,* said the actor, *to yield oneself up to the forest,* that had always been his ideal—to become part of nature oneself. *The forest, the virgin forest, the life of a woodcutter— that has always been my ideal,* he said with sudden excitement, as he made to leave. Although everyone had drunk a good deal, the only person who was totally drunk as the party broke up was Auersberger; this was how it had been thirty, twenty-five and twenty years earlier. Slumped in his chair, he was unaware that all the guests were now standing up and about to take their leave. As I stood up myself, I recalled hearing the actor utter the words *the forest, the virgin forest, the life of a woodcutter* earlier in the evening, once during dinner, as he was eating his pike, and again in the music room, though at the time I had not known what he meant. Much of the time my attention had naturally been concentrated not on him, but on Jeannie Billroth; all through supper I had hardly taken my eyes off her, paying no attention to what the actor was saying most of the time, catching only the odd half sentence, never a full sentence. During the meal I had not been in the least interested in what he had to say; it was only much later, in the music room, after he had drunk more than was really good for him, that he began to interest me, because he had meanwhile become a different person, as it now strikes me. Everything he had said in the dining room was drivel, the kind of vacuous small talk we are accustomed to hearing from aging or aged actors, whom I always try to avoid because I cannot endure their conversation, and because the so-called wisdom of old age they purvey, which is in fact merely the crass imbecility of old age, grates on my nerves. I have repeatedly been struck by this and have accordingly always taken care to avoid such people's company. But after a few glasses of wine a change had come over this actor from the Burgtheater: all at once he had become an interesting person, with a philosophical cast of mind that suddenly revealed itself when he uttered the words *the forest, the virgin forest, the life of a woodcutter*. I have since learned that these are catchwords used by many others like him, by millions of others. At the end of this *artistic dinner* I suddenly became aware of what the actor meant by using these catchwords, what he was trying to say to himself and others, what he was trying to tell all of us, and I began to listen to him attentively. It seems to me that this man, who started off by being merely tiresome and uninteresting, was transformed for a brief spell into an interesting person, a person who—if only for this brief spell—was able to capture my attention. Suddenly I was no longer interested in anything Jeannie Billroth or Anna Schreker had to say, but only in what the actor from the Burgtheater was saying. And so I turned my attention away from them and the other people present at this *artistic dinner*, whom I had found uninteresting right from the beginning. I haven't listened to the others at all, I thought, I haven't even heard what little they've had to say. This man, who had at first seemed merely a portentous driveler, seeking to create an effect with his feeble jokes and stale anecdotes, had in the course of this *artistic dinner* turned into a fascinating figure, even a *philosophical figure*, I thought. This is not, I think, a phenomenon that we observe in many people, though it may now and then be observed in the old: at first they appear as portentous drivelers, distasteful purveyors of jokes and anecdotes, putting on the act of the typical Viennese with artistic or intellectual pretensions, but then they undergo a truly philosophical metamorphosis in the course of an evening, in the course of a dinner like this *artistic dinner* given by the Auersbergers in the Gentzgasse: at first they strike us as ludicrously inflated and inane, but then, when they have had a few drinks—usually more than is good for them—they are suddenly able to convert our initial aversion into genuine liking by bringing a certain spiritual or even philosophical element into play. It seems to me that when the actor first made his appearance he was playing his accustomed role as the actor from the Burgtheater, and it was as the actor from the Burgtheater—a figure that I found quite repellent—that he later addressed himself to the *genuine pike*, continuing his Burgtheater performance throughout the pike-eating ceremony. But then, having finished with the pike and had two or three cigars and a few glasses of white wine, he suddenly became a thinking human being, even a philosopher of sorts, transforming himself from a gargoyle into a philosophical human being, from a repellent stage character into a real person. This is the converse of the normal process: usually people begin by behaving like human beings, but eventually, after a certain amount of eating and drinking, they turn into gargoyles, being unable to do otherwise. This is what we observe every day: we meet people at parties who become progressively more repulsive until they finally turn into gargoyles, and, as the evening wears on and increasing quantities of food and drink are consumed, the whole company becomes increasingly repellent. That night, however, the Burgtheater actor went through the reverse process, transforming himself from a gargoyle into a philosophically minded human being, if not from a driveler into a philosopher. In the end I found myself *enthralled,* as they say, by this man, whom I had for so long found quite distasteful and whose demeanor had aroused in me not merely indignation, but anger; I was now *no longer angry and indignant, but enthralled*, unlike Jeannie Billroth, who I think was enthralled by him at first, but gradually became infuriated during the pike-eating ceremony, and in the end detested him. I ended up by being enthralled by the actor from the Burgtheater, Jeannie Billroth by detesting him, I think, and that says it all. The way he said *the forest, the virgin forest, the life of a woodcutter* was not, I think, symptomatic of senile sentimentality, but of mental clarity. And the way he countered Jeannie's attack appears to me as anything but senile, anything but a resort to the opportunism of old age. We sit through an interminable supper party with one of these artistic nonentities that pullulate in Vienna, one of these atrocious pseudo-artists of whom we know hundreds —these unappetizing painters and sculptors and writers and musicians and actors, these horrendous provincial artists who converge on Vienna in droves—and as if this were not enough, we find that the person sitting opposite us during this appalling, interminable supper at the Auersbergers', which we would have done well to miss, is an actor from the Burgtheater, the very prototype, it seems to me, of the Viennese pseudo-artist. Then suddenly we observe that this man, who began by making the most distasteful exhibition of himself and filling us with the utmost revulsion, has been transformed into someone with a philosophical turn of mind who actually interests us, into what might be called a *momentary philosopher*, who is able to arouse our interest. It is clearly not true that all old people are philosophers, and I know of nothing so foolish as the proposition that this is so, but old people do have a philosophical propensity: they all have the potential to become philosophers, or at any rate to philosophize, if only for a few moments, just as the actor from the Burgtheater, during the course of this *artistic dinner*, was prompted, by whatever motives, to philosophize for a few moments, to become a *momentary philosopher*. Next morning, with the return of sobriety, the momentary philosopher no doubt reverts to being the insufferable stage character with whom we first became acquainted. It was precisely a party like this one in the Gentzgasse that produced this effect on him, I thought, transforming him for a few brief moments into a philosopher, though naturally it had no such effect on the others, for nothing could *ever* have a philosophical impact on them. Not on the Auersbergers, not on Anna Schreker, and certainly not on the other guests—especially not on the two young writers, whose age alone precludes them from what we may call the philosophical condition. I believe that to qualify for this condition one needs to have an *experience of life that goes some way back into history and is constantly informed by history;* this qualification was possessed by the actor from the Burgtheater, as it is by all old people, and above all by the very old. During the course of my life I think I have become more interested in the old and the very old than in the young; more and more I have sought out the company of the old and the very old and spent more and more of my time with them, rather than with the young. After all, I knew about youth when I myself was young, but not about old age: hence it was old age that interested me, not youth. *Get all you can out of the old,* I always told myself, and indeed I always derived the greatest benefit from following this precept; I have no hesitation in saying that I derived immense profit from it. Old age always attracted my curiosity, I think, whereas youth never did, because I knew it at first hand. The Burgtheater actor, I believe, is a person who constantly suppresses his propensity to philosophy, which has evolved during the course of his life—which means during the course of his own history, our history, everyone's history. Hence most of the time we have dealings with people who suppress their philosophical propensity until it atrophies and dies. Only occasionally do we have an opportunity to *discern* this propensity in them, as I discerned it in the actor at this supper party, though I suspect he did not discern it in himself and was probably quite *unaware* of it. All at once I was fascinated by the way he uttered the words *the forest, the virgin forest, the life of a woodcutter,* and then repeated them several times. But this does not mean that I should take to him now, were I to meet him again. He remains for me the unattractive and essentially superficial stage character he was from the start. I was revolted by the way he took his leave, kissing the hostess's hand in his *Viennese Burgtheater manner.* And when he paid Jeannie Billroth a compliment—a foolish and entirely unnecessary compliment, an insolent compliment in fact—by telling her, as he kissed her hand too, that he liked her *intellectual audacity*—he actually said, *I like your intellectual audacity* —he had once more reverted to type and become the distasteful stage character that he had been at the outset. I too had drunk more than was good for me, I think, but not as much as the actor, to say nothing of Auersberger, who did not wake up until the guests had all left. The two young writers, who had talked about nothing but how rebellious they were, though without being able to say what they were rebelling against, were also completely drunk and had difficulty getting to their feet. In the end the Burgtheater actor was the only one who still had the strength and the poise to make a decent exit from the Gentzgasse—and, I may add, with the utmost politeness—for none of the others was in a fit condition to do so. *What an excellent pike that was!* he finally said to Auersberger's wife, after which he was the first to leave, walking alone down the stairs in the entrance hall. He's not even unsure on his feet, I thought, watching him from the door of the apartment as he descended the stairs. It is one of my principles that I like to leave a party alone, and so I waited with Auersberger's wife at the door of the apartment until all the others had gone down the stairs. Yes, it's been a sad day, hasn't it? I said to her after they had all left, referring once more to Joana. Perhaps it was best that she killed herself, I said, it was *probably* the best time for her to go. I was aware of how embarrassing and distasteful this remark was, a remark that is frequently made when somebody has committed suicide. We want to say something appropriate, I thought at that moment, and then we say something entirely inappropriate, something distasteful and stupid. What would she have had to look forward to? I said, adding yet another embarrassing and distasteful remark to the first. Everyone should act as they think fit, I went on, which again was embarrassing and distasteful. So it was best to say no more. I ran down the stairs as if I were twenty years younger, suddenly taking two, three, or even four steps at a time. In the entrance hall below I told myself that it had been ridiculous to kiss her forehead as I left. Like thirty years ago, I thought, just as ridiculous as it was thirty years ago. I had kissed her on the forehead as I used to do in the fifties, and this fact annoyed me all the way from the Gentzgasse to the city. I haven't seen her for twenty years, and I have to admit that fundamentally I hate her, yet when I leave I have to go and kiss her forehead! But it was only her forehead you kissed, *at least it was only her forehead*, I kept on telling myself as I walked through the city, which was still dark, feeling angry with myself. If only I'd left with the others I'd have been spared this embarrassment, I thought, but I didn't want to leave with the others, above all because I wanted to avoid an encounter with Jeannie, especially in the street, and especially now, for I'd have been sure to have a terrible row with her, I'd have been bound to say *too much*, to make *too many reproaches*, to cause her *too much offense*, I thought. And she'd have done the same, and so it was as well to stay behind and let the others go on ahead. Being alone with Auersberger's wife was certainly more tolerable than being alone with Jeannie, I thought; to be alone in the street with Jeannie would have been disastrous, I thought, whereas to be alone with Auersberger's wife at the door of their apartment was at least endurable. But I now re-proached myself for having given her a kiss on the fore-head, after twenty years, perhaps even twenty-two or twenty-three years, during which I had positively hated her, with the same hatred that I had felt for her husband; and

I reproached myself too for having lied to her, saying that her *artistic dinner* had given me *great pleasure*, when in fact I had found it nothing short of revolting. To get ourselves out of a tight spot, it seems to me, we are ourselves just as mendacious as those we are always accusing of mendacity, those whom we despise and drag in the dirt for their mendacity; we are not one jot better than the people we constantly find objectionable and insufferable, those repellent people with whom we want to have as few dealings as possible, though, if we are honest, we do have dealings with them and are no different from them. We reproach them with all kinds of objectionable and insufferable behavior and are no less insufferable and objectionable ourselves—perhaps we are even more insufferable and objectionable, it occurs to me. I told her I was glad to have renewed my ties with her and her husband, to have visited them again in the Gentzgasse after twenty years, and as I said this I thought what a vile hypocrite I was, recoiling from nothing, not even the basest lie. Standing at the door of the apartment, I told her that I had liked the actor from the Burgtheater, that I had liked Anna Schreker, even that I had liked the two young writers; I said all this as I watched the others going down the stairs, all the time thinking how revolting they were, yet at the same time telling her how much I had liked them all. To think that I am capable of such base hypocrisy, I thought as I was speaking to her—to think that I am capable of quite openly lying to her face, that I am capable of telling her to her face the precise opposite of what I feel, because it makes things momentarily more endurable! I also told her that I was sorry not to have heard her sing one of the *Purcell arias that she used to sing so beautifully, so superbly, so incomparably,* and that I was sorry above all that I had been out of touch with her and her husband for twenty years—which was another piece of mendacity, one of my basest and most contemptible lies. I even said that I particularly regretted that Joana could not have been present that evening, and that she would probably have wished us—that is, the Auersbergers and myself —to renew our contacts, now that I was back from London for some time, though not for good. We would *keep up* our contacts from now on, I said untruthfully, hearing the others leave the building as I still stood at the top of the stairs. *Joana had to die, she had to kill herself, so that we could get together* again, I told her, after which I briefly embraced her and kissed her on the forehead, then ran down the stairs and out into the street. In every street I walked along I was tormented by the thought that everything I had said to her was a lie, that I had been consciously lying with every word I had spoken. For the truth is that after this *artistic dinner* I still hated her as much as ever, her and her husband, the *Novalis of sound*, the successor of Webern who had got stuck in the fifties. Perhaps I hated them now with an even more intense hatred than before— with the *Auersberger hatred* that I have borne them for twenty years, it now occurs to me—because twenty years ago they went behind my back and slandered me so viciously, seizing every opportunity to denigrate me and run me down to all and sundry after I had left them— simply to save myself from being devoured by them. They always asserted, and still assert, that *I turned my back on them, not they on me*, just as for twenty years they have asserted that *I* took advantage of them, that *they* supported me, that *they* kept me alive, when the truth is that *I kept them alive*, that *I saved them*, that it was *I* who supported them—not with money, of course, but with all my talents. I ran through the streets as though I were running away from a nightmare, running faster and faster toward the Inner City, not knowing why I was running in that direction, since to get home I would have had to go in the opposite direction, but perhaps I did not want to go home. If only I'd spent this winter in London! I said to myself. It was four in the morning, and I was running in the direction of the Inner City when I should have been going home. I should have stayed in London at all costs, I told myself, and I kept on running in the direction of the Inner City, without knowing why, and I told myself that London had always brought me happiness and Vienna unhappiness, and I went on running, running, running, as though now, in the eighties, I was once more running away from the fifties, running into the eighties, the dangerous, benighted, mindless eighties, and again it struck me that instead of going to this tasteless *artistic dinner* I ought to have read my Gogol or my Pascal or my Montaigne, and as I ran it seemed to me that I was running away from the Auersberger nightmare, and with ever greater energy I ran away from the Auersberger nightmare and toward the Inner City, and as I ran I reflected that the city through which I was running, dreadful though I had always felt it to be and still felt it to be, was still the best city there was, that Vienna, which I found detestable and had always found detestable, was suddenly once again the best city in the world, my own city, my beloved Vienna, and that these people, whom I had always hated and still hated and would go on hating, were still the best people in the world: I hated them, yet found them somehow touching—I hated Vienna, yet found it somehow touching—I cursed these people, yet could not help loving them—I hated Vienna yet could not help loving it. And now, as I ran through the streets of the Inner City, I thought: This is my city and always will be my city, these are my people and always will be my people, and as I went on running, I thought: I've survived this dreadful *artistic dinner*, just as I've survived all the other horrors. I'll write about this *artistic dinner* in the Gentzgasse, I thought, without knowing what I would write—simply that I would write *something* about it. And as I went on running I thought: I'll write something *at once*, no matter what— I'll write about this *artistic dinner* in the Gentzgasse *at once, now. Now*, I thought—*at once*, I told myself over and over again as I ran through the Inner City—*at once*, I told myself, *now—at once, at once*, before it's too late.

Thomas Bernhard was born in 1931 and grew up in Salzburg and in Vienna, where he studied music. In 1957 he began a second career as a playwright, poet, and novelist. The winner of the three most distinguished and coveted literary prizes awarded in Germany, he has become one of the most widely translated and admired writers of his generation. His works already published in English include the novels *Gargoyles*, *The Lime Works*, *Correction*, and *Concrete*, and a memoir, *Gathering Evidence*. A number of his plays have been produced off-Broadway and at the Tyrone Guthrie Theatre in Minneapolis, and at theaters in London and throughout Europe.